On Viney's Mountain

Barn Loom

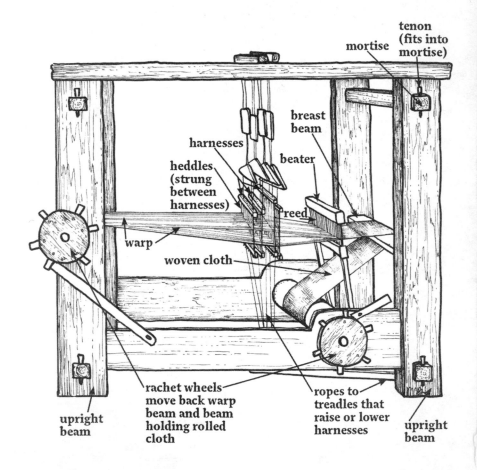

tenon (fits into mortise)

mortise

breast beam

harnesses

heddles (strung between harnesses)

beater

reed

warp

woven cloth

rachet wheels move back warp beam and beam holding rolled cloth

ropes to treadles that raise or lower harnesses

upright beam

upright beam

On Viney's Mountain

Joan Donaldson

Holiday House / New York

Copyright © 2009 by Joan Donaldson
All Rights Reserved
Holiday House is registered in the U.S. Patent and Trademark Office.
Printed in the United States of America
www.holidayhouse.com
First Edition
1   3   5   7   9   10   8   6   4   2

Frontispiece drawing by Margo Carlson Berke

Library of Congress Cataloging-in-Publication Data

Donaldson, Joan.
On Viney's mountain / by Joan Donaldson.—1st ed.
p. cm.
Summary: In the Cumberland Mountains during the fall of 1879, sixteen-year-old Viney is
shocked to hear that Englishmen will arrive on her mountain and build a new community,
massacring the beautiful area that inspires her weaving designs.
ISBN 978-0-8234-2129-9 (hardcover)
[1. Weaving—Fiction.   2. Mountain life—Tennessee—Fiction.
3. Family life—Tennessee—Fiction.   4. Rugby (Tenn.)—History—
19th century—Fiction.]   I. Title.
PZ7.D714985On 2009
[Fic]—dc22
2009001062

For Carol Coleman
and
Donna Slone,
my two favorite mountain women

Acknowledgements

My abundant thanks to the many individuals
who helped create this story.

To Eric Wilson and Vi Behl, who introduced my family to Historic
Rugby; without their constant supply of books, microfilm, interviews, and
general encouragement, this book would not have been written.

To Julie Amper, for her wisdom, attention to details, and gracious editing.

To Regina Griffin, who accepted the manuscript
and offered early encouragement.

To Barbara Stagg, director of Historic Rugby,
for additional historic information.

To the Firekeepers, Karmen Kooyers, Judi Boogaart, Patricia Trattles,
Pam Eicher, and Betsy Kaylor, who supported me along the way.

To John Van Voorhees, my husband, who cheers me on
and tolerates living with a writer.

To Sena Jeter Naslund, Cathleen Medwick and George Getschow,
Robin Heald, and Jenn Sherlock, who gave me faith in my talent.

To Cindy Amneus at the Cincinnati Art Museum,
who showed me Dicey Fletcher's weaving.

To Donna Slone, James Goode, and Carol Coleman,
for their information about Appalachian culture, especially to Carol
for her connections with Rugby.

To Margo Carlson Berke, for researching and drawing the loom illustration.

And thanks be to God for this incredible gift.

Chapter One

October 1879,
Cumberland Mountains of Tennessee

What you have to do is to discover someplace
on the face of this broad planet where you may
set to work on the best conditions; where the old blunders
have the smallest chance of repeating themselves.

THOMAS HUGHES

I was about halfway up the ridge, picking pokeberries, when I spied the foreigners. The two men rode their horses to the edge of a small clearing and began to climb toward me. The trail was slick from wet leaves and littered with bits of shale. My own bare feet had slipped on the acorns scattered about, but such bountiful mast would fatten our hogs, which ran wild in these woods. Leaves fluttered and swirled about the men, sifting through branches like yellow and red snowflakes.

Both men wore cravats and shiny black leather boots, and one sported a silk top hat. I had read about rich gentlemen in Charles Dickens's books. When these fellars spoke, the words were in English, but they had same peculiar accent as our Amos Hill, who hailed from that land ruled by Queen Victoria.

I hid behind a laurel bush and eavesdropped. The men kept squinting up at the treetops, mumbling about board feet and writing down notes. I didn't have a peace about those strangers. A year or so back, a dozen Yankees came down from Boston and bought this land. Set to cutting the tallest of our trees. I cried whenever I watched a smooth-skinned beech fall and cursed their crosscut saws as they severed our oaks. After a year of timbering, the Yankees had loaded their wagons and rumbled away. Now it seemed these Englishmen wanted the remaining lumber.

Picking up my basket, I lit out for Aunt Alta and Aunt Idy's cabin. They live apiece down the trail near the top of the ridge. Usually I take time to relish the trip down this path, bordered with straight hemlocks and silvery beech trees, but today the notion of losing those trees gave wings to my feet. A patch of lumpy gray clouds, like a dirty fleece, slid across the sun. Aunt Alta was on her porch spinning with her great wheel.

"Aunt Alta!" I cried. "I just spied foreigners on the ridge, down by the clearing, and they kept pointing at our timber. I'll die if'n they cut more of our trees."

Aunt Alta never missed a lick, walking backward as the yarn spun out of the locks held in her fingers, and then moving forward, winding the yarn onto the spindle. Her thin gray hair was pulled back into a bun, and she wore a dress dyed butternut brown.

"Were they marrying age, Viney?"

"Aunt Alta! One's old enough to be my pa, and the other could be my grandpa!"

"Pity. Weaving is honorable work, Viney, but you being sixteen, it's time you be shut of your unseemly ways and wed. Look at your sister! Lizzie could pick any fellar on the ridge."

I wanted to roll my eyes, but I knew better than to sass Aunt Alta, who had mothered me since Pa had left. My sister chased anything in britches.

"Well, ma'am, I reckon that between you and the Good Lord, one of you will find me a husband. We don't need foreigners invading our hills, robbing us of land and lumber."

"Not much came of those Yankee settlers. Took what they came for and lit out. I reckon little will come from these men either."

I was fixing to leave when Aunt Idy appeared, toting two buckets of water. I ran and carried them back to the cabin. "If I'd known you were at the spring, Aunt Idy, I'd have fetched those for you."

"I know you would've, Viney." Aunt Idy eyed the two of us. "What's all the fuss about?"

"Viney saw foreigners on the ridge, but they're not of marrying age," Aunt Alta said.

"Your brother, Jacob, talked to those men," Aunt Idy said. "They've come to start a settlement. Seems an Englishman named Hughes wants to bring over a boatload of lads and turn them into farmers."

Aunt Alta laid off spinning and started to grin. "Praise the Lord," she crooned. "Maybe He'll send someone our highfalutin niece will cozy up to."

I could feel the words boiling inside me, but I bit my tongue. "I best be going," I said.

Back at our cabin, I dumped the pokeberries into a

crock and poured water and vinegar over the fruit to produce a maroon dye. I'd allow a day or two for the color to leach from the berries before I dyed my wool. Setting a plate for a lid on the crock, I shoved it into a corner. I didn't want Jacob thinking this was a new recipe for switchel.

I could hear Jacob calling to his team of mules while he plowed. The wind was from that direction, and I felt colder air moving in. If it cleared, we'd have frost tonight.

I set to sweeping. Sweeping and chopping wood are the best labors for a riled mind. I brushed away cobwebs and cleaned beneath our beds. Smacking the woven rugs, I sent dirt across the floor and out the door. I imagined the tumbling dust balls to be Aunt Alta's words.

"If'n you hanker after a man so much, fetch one into your own cabin, Aunt Alta. I've no need for tobacco juice on my floor or waiting to eat until his 'lordship' finishes his dinner. I like my food hot!" I swept the dirt onto the porch and off the steps. "Send me a man who will treat me like I'm worth more than a mule, and I might pay him some mind." With one final whack, I watched the breeze pick up the dust and scatter it across the path.

A redbird flitted between the golden sassafras leaves. I wished someday I could discover the right plant to yield such a vivid red. I'd heard tell of the shell of a bug that was used to dye the robes of kings scarlet. Someday when I had cash money, I aimed to send to Knoxville for some of those bug shells and weave me a red coverlet. I gazed at my own first love, rising mighty and noble in the west corner of our cabin.

No man could match my loom for beauty or provide the excitement of watching warp and weft grow into cloth. Jacob and I felled the maples for the loom's uprights. With my own hands I scraped the bark off the logs with a drawknife, while Jacob squared them with his ax. The feel and smell of wood tickled me almost as much as wool. Using a chisel and mallet, we formed the mortise and tenons that linked the timber frame together.

Jacob and I fashioned the harness frame, and I knotted the many heddles from strong flax thread I'd spun. Each time I stepped on a treadle, the harnesses rose true, not lopsided. When I walloped the beater against the weft, the legs of my loom stood firm and did not travel across the floor. I ran my hand along the breast beam. My loom was my young'uns and man all woven into one.

Singing drifted in through the open doorway, and I spied Lizzie carrying a basket of walnuts. My sister had a voice like a thrush and only had to hear a tune once and it rested in her memory. Songs sprang from her lips from morning to candlelight.

"The cuckoo she's a pretty bird, she sings as she flies,
She brings us glad tidings and she tells us no lies . . ."

She only sang that song after seeing her Lucas, and I could tell by her walk that she had spent the afternoon with him. Framed by the gourd vines climbing up the porch railings, she was a lovely sight, with black curls framing her face. She paused and sniffed one of the late roses that had opened this morning.

"How's Lucas?"

"Sweeter than sorghum." Lizzie hung her sunbonnet on

its peg. She always wore her bonnet to protect her precious complexion, but I like to feel the sun on my face.

"He picked up the walnuts while you sweet-talked him, didn't he?" I pointed to her fingers. "Your hands are still white as lard."

"The trouble with you, Viney, is that you don't know how to manage men. You see them as a threat to your freedom and your clean floor. I see them as useful."

"I'd like to hear you repeat that after you wed and are puking before breakfast."

She snorted. "I don't aim for that to happen until I can find me a man who can take me off this ridge and give me what I want. I'll have maids to care for me."

"Well, a whole passel of Englishmen is coming." The way she tilted her head turned my stomach. Poor Lucas.

"Do tell." She leaned back against the porch railing and smiled that wicked little grin. She filled her red calico dress in a pert sort of way. Just the right curves to alter a man's step. Boys knew better than to pay me any mind, but they kept their eyes on Lizzie.

"Aunt Idy and Jacob know more. The gents are starting a settlement."

Lizzie frowned. "But I want a man to carry me off to a town, not stay in these hills. Why would any gentleman want to live here?"

"A few winks from you, and I reckon you could convince one of them to buy you a house in Knoxville." I grinned. She lobbed a walnut at me and shrieked when the juice stained her fingers.

Chapter Two

At twenty, a mountain woman is old in all
that makes a woman old—toil, sorrow,
childbearing, loneliness and pitiful want.

Emma Bell Miles, *The Spirit of the Mountains*

For weeks life kept me busy cutting corn, stacking fodder shocks, and drying apples, then we commenced slaughtering Jacob's hogs and filled the smokehouse with pork. Even Lizzie dipped her slim fingers in mounds of sausage and stuffed it into crocks that we stored in the springhouse.

About that time the fall rains set in, and while I hankered to visit Mr. and Mrs. Hill, I had no desire to wade the muddy trails. Instead I burned out the centers of corncobs and wound the cob spools with yarn. Jacob carried my warping board onto the porch, and I walked back and forth, drawing yarn off the spools. I liked listening to the spools rattle as they rolled on the rack. They beat out their own tune like dancing feet. I removed the yarn from the warping board by using my hand like a crochet hook and looped that yarn into a loose chain that I draped over my loom. 'Twas an odd sight. Masses of curly hair cascading off the main beam. The rain drumming on the cedar shakes filled the air with moisture, which made the yarn fuzzy. The limp wool gave off a harsh smell from the alum and copper sulfate mordants that burned the inside of my nose. I didn't mind such tedious work because it gave a body time to think. Now that the trees had shucked their leaves, I could see the bones of the ridge. I know God made these hills, but how? Did He sweep the dirt from digging the seas into high piles? Where did the clouds come from?

Finally one clear morning in December, the muddy ground froze solid. Lizzie and I drew on our shawls and stepped out into a brilliant world. Hoar frost glistened on each twig and stalk. A sight so mortal sweet that it hurt to breathe. How I wish I could weave frost patterns into my coverlets like the ice edging the curled laurel leaves.

Lizzie sauntered on ahead, but my boots bit my feet. I hated wearing shoes, plaguey things that squished my toes, but the frozen ground would numb my feet. I carried two of the Hills' books in my basket.

When we arrived, Mr. Hill was in his barn tending his sheep. Great, round woolly balls, they ran from Lizzie and me and clustered behind Mr. Hill. The barn smelled thickly of dung, hay, and wool.

"Good morning, ladies," Mr. Hill shouted over the bleating of the sheep. "How fine to view your faces this frosty morning."

"Morning, Mr. Hill. I'm a-needing some merino wool," I said. "Have you any fleece saved back?" His ragged Cotswold sheep, all covered with ringlets, moved toward us. I love to sink my fingers into their long locks and feel the rich grease that softened the skin. Mr. Hill sprinkled a little salt on the ground near our feet, and those sheep nearly hugged us, they were so excited to lick it up.

"I believe Mrs. Hill kept some. Please come inside." He closed the barn door behind us and escorted Lizzie and me to his cabin.

The Hills had come from England years ago and settled in Michigan before heading south. They had brought fine ways to our mountains, but never acted uppity. Their thick Brussels carpet covered the well-scrubbed floor, and a cookstove radiated heat while the blue and white china sparkled in the cupboard. After a visit to the Hills, Lizzie usually put on airs for days, like she was the one born across the waters.

Mrs. Hill held out her hands. "My dears! How good of you to call. Shall you stay for tea? I baked shortbread this morning."

"Yes, ma'am," I answered. Lizzie was busy studying the lace doily on a little round table. A basket of knitting wires and fine thread rested on the doily. Persnickety sort of lady's work, knitting lace would suit Lizzie.

"Did you keep back any merino, Mum?" Mr. Hill hung his tweed vest on a peg. Mrs. Hill set a kettle on the stove and went to a basket in a corner.

"A bit is left. Perhaps this spring, Viney, you could come help at lambing time and earn yourself a lamb. Then you could have your own supply of wool."

Mr. Hill stuffed the fleece in a small muslin poke and handed it to me. "April will bring more than lambs this year. Mr. Hughes writes that the first crew of settlers should arrive in the spring. About a dozen lads. Even a few lasses will join them in June."

Appeared Lizzie would have to move swiftly if she was to snag one of the lads before their own women interfered with her plans. She cocked her head in that aggravating way, showing off her slim neck. "Then you know the settlers, Mr. Hill?"

"No, Miss Lizzie, not personally. But everyone in England recognizes Mr. Hughes's name. He's not just a famous author, he also helped form some of the first labor movements. Hughes sent the men who came last fall; they asked me if I would advise the settlers."

"And what will they build? Houses for the gentlemen?" Lizzie helped herself to a wedge of shortbread while Mrs. Hill poured tea.

"Not at first, miss. Just a few cabins. The lads are coming to learn to farm."

Poor Lizzie. Only more farmers to court her. I could have cackled over the pitiful look that swept across her face. Even Mrs. Hill smiled.

"The young gentlemen wish to learn trades. To work with their hands. Their parents will provide them an allowance. I suppose to you it would seem a fortune." Mrs. Hill patted Lizzie's hand. "But come summer, the Land Board plans to erect a large inn where the ladies or families can stay. A summer place. They hope the earnings from the inn will help support the colony."

"Laws! An inn! How fine." Lizzie's eyes glinted. "What's a land board?" She poured cream into her tea.

I watched the current of cream swirl through the dark tea. Even the term *land board* sounded flat and ugly.

"The Land Board consists of wealthy Englishmen who

are investing money in the colony. They bought the Yankees' land, and will divide it into plots and sell it to the settlers. Those two men who visited were members of the board. Most of them will remain in London, but a few of the investors will visit now and then." Mr. Hill stirred his tea.

I could feel Lizzie begin to purr. Rich men coming to the ridge. I wanted to gag.

After tea Lizzie asked Mrs. Hill to teach her how to knit lace, while Mr. Hill and I discussed Mr. Dickens's *Oliver Twist*, then he gave me *Tom Brown's School Days* by Mr. Hughes to take home. When the shadows stretched across the room, Lizzie and I hugged Mrs. Hill and walked home.

January brought deep snow. In the dim winter light I squinted at the thread of my warp and drew it through the rows of heddles with a hook. I had heard folks grumbling about warping a loom, but to me, warping was akin to churning butter or chopping wood. Once I found that inner rhythm, like the beat of a reel played over and over, I drifted away. I drew through a dozen yarn ends and rested my eyes. Slowly the web grew across my loom until all the strands were firmly knotted to the front and back bars.

Come early February, the tips of the maple branches reddened, though the snow lingered on the northern slopes. The angle of the sun grew higher, and from sheltered spots I picked dandelion greens for our dinners. I fastened the weaving draft for "Pine Burst" onto the beater of my loom. Some folks say weaving patterns look like chicken tracks inked on paper, but drafts are like the music printed in Mrs. Hill's hymnbook. Just as those notes spelled out a tune, I could read the light and dark markings and secure the correct tie-up of the pedals for creating that pattern.

It's always a wonder to watch how raising and lowering threads by changing the combination of pedals can create patterns of roses, wheels, or waves. It takes both the ups and downs to form a coverlet pattern, and I reckon that in this world each of us rides a heddle, weaving our own design out of the joys and sorrows given us.

Some days, moments still pinched me when I wished I'd known Mama and could have watched her weave. Or I wondered where Pa went and if he still lived. But I'd shake myself free from the pinching and find comfort in listening to Lizzie sing while she knitted lace. Sometimes I joined in, and she would draw out harmonies. I would grip my beater, and a glorious feeling would rise over me as I watched a pattern form.

CHAPTER THREE

To give the young settler a fair chance of finding his legs . . .
we provide him barrack room at a cheap rate, & have
arranged that all the work on our unsold land
shall be done by such settlers.

THOMAS HUGHES

In late March the Hills sent for me. Lambing had started.

"Tain't fair, you get to go. You'd rather sleep under one of your coverlets than beneath Mrs. Hill's lace spread." Arms crossed, Lizzie stood in the doorway. "She knit almost a hundred squares of real lace and sewed them together."

"Might be Mr. Hill reckons you'll swoon at the sight of blood. Lambing's bloody. Just like women giving birth." I brushed past Lizzie.

Her face paled. "Ain't fit talk for a lady. I pity the Hills having to put up with you!" Lizzie slammed the door and set the floorboards quaking.

The grass crunched beneath my boots, and the air was as crisp as starched linen sheets. A red-tail hawk lifted his wings and rose into the sky. Folks say redtails steal chickens, but they never bother my birds. Their shriek matches the spirit of these hills.

I knocked on the Hill's door and wiped my feet before entering.

"Morning, ma'am." Mrs. Hill stood at the table cutting out the biscuits she called scones.

"Mercy, you startled me. Have you had your breakfast?"

"Yes, ma'am. Should I head to the barn?"

"Yes. Amos has been up all night. He'll be relieved to see you. Here, take that bucket of water warming on the hearth. The ewes will appreciate it."

"Yes, ma'am." I set my basket on a low bench. "Bye for now."

I marched to the barn and found Mr. Hill dozing in a splint-bottom chair. Some of the splints had cracked along the edges, and the woven seat sagged.

"Morning, sir. Mrs. Hill sent me out." Mr. Hill shook himself and yawned.

"Ah, yes, morning. Was a long night. Molly and Polly lambed. Two sets of twins. Sally and Sue had twins. Now Betsy and Minnie show signs they'll be next."

"What sort of signs, sir?" The round ewes all looked the same, like hairy snowballs.

"Pawing the ground. Bleating. I separated them into this stall. Remember, feet and noses come first. Clear the lamb's nose of mucus, but let the mama lick him. I won't be long." Mr. Hill trudged back toward the house.

I knew enough to check the water buckets and fluff the hay in the mangers for the other sheep. Cobwebs fluttered like gray curtains in the barn's corners. They were good for stopping bleeding, but I hoped we'd not need them. I settled onto a mound of straw nearby one of the ewes that lay on her side, panting and moaning. I rubbed her belly.

"Reckon, even in your world the women do all the work. Hope you see what dallying with a ram cost you."

The ewe bleated, gazing up at me with frightened eyes. I rambled on, hoping to calm her.

"But I suppose a ram's life is not much better. Breeding in the fall and into the stewpot for the winter." I could see the tiny hooves showing, and knelt next to her. "Push, mama, push!" The ewe grunted and the baby's head appeared. Behind me the other ewe bawled.

"Laws!" She was birthing, too. I checked the lamb's position, but faster than a cricket, that old sheep pushed out one lamb and then another. She commenced licking and crooning to her babies. I gave her the bucket of warm water. Birthing made that ewe thirsty.

When the first ewe finished, triplets squirmed on the straw. I wiped away some of the slime that slicked their bodies while their mother nuzzled and licked them. They tried to walk and find their ma's udder, but their thin legs sprawled out and sent them tumbling. I could feel the lamb's heartbeat when I helped one latch on to a teat. Pride bloomed inside me, and I reckon this was how a new mother felt about her babe.

I relished that month with the Hills. Mr. Hill said I brought a blessing to the farm, and he gave me two lambs, which I named David and Baasheepa. Jacob fetched over my wheel so I could spin in the evenings while Mr. Hill read to us from a book by a Russian named Tolstoy. Once, I came upon Mrs. Hill fingering a hank of yarn I had plied.

"So fine. So even. How I wish I had your talent," she murmured.

I blushed and hastened off, but her praise rose inside me like yeast bubbling in sat-rising bread.

One afternoon Mr. Ramsey, who lived near the Hills, reined in his team and dropped off a letter. The stamp said England, and in thick script Thomas Hughes had written his address on the back of the envelope. I wanted to wad it up and throw it down the well, but I dutifully laid it on the kitchen table.

After supper Mr. Hill leaned back in his chair, lifting the front legs off the floor.

"Amos . . . " Mrs. Hill began. *Kathunk*, the legs hit the floor.

"Thomas says the first lot of lads should arrive in less than a month. He is not coming until fall, and asked if I would accept being the man in charge of the settlement."

"But your farmwork?" Mrs. Hill started clearing the table, and I jumped up to help.

"Several lads can divide their time between here and the building. We'll manage."

"Where will the lads stay?"

"In tents erected on wooden platforms. The first buildings we construct will be boardinghouses, then the inn for the ladies and guests."

I commenced wiping the table, where in less than a month a group of those Englishmen would be sitting. There was nothing I could do to stop it.

On the day I was to go home, I heard a far off rumbling, but there were no storm clouds gathering. The thundering swelled until I could pick out the banging of wooden wheels on rocks, cows bellowing, and men shouting. The very ground beneath my feet vibrated. I ran out to the road and froze.

Fourteen teams of oxen plodded toward me, each pulling a loaded wagon or a stoneboat piled with supplies. Teamsters shouted commands and flicked their whips over the beasts' heads. Now and then one of the bullocks would swipe at a low branch and pull down a mouthful. The smell of cattle and sweat flooded over me.

Mr. and Mrs. Hill joined me. "A bit early," Mr. Hill commented.

I recognized the mountaineers driving the teams, but a half a dozen foreign lads in highfalutin garb walked between the wagons. I studied their faces. One boy scowled at me, but the black-haired boy driving a wagon kept his eyes down. Another lad with auburn hair almost tripped he was so busy staring at the Hills and me. I felt my heart sour like day-old milk. Wouldn't Lizzie be green when she learned that I had spied the gentlemen first.

Chapter Four

We who live so far apart . . . are never at ease without the feel of the forest on every side. . . . The nature of the mountaineer demands that he have solitude for the unhampered growth of his personality, wing room for his eagle heart.

EMMA BELL MILES, *The Spirit of the Mountains*

*L*izzie sat churning and drilling questions into me like a woodpecker attacks a dead tree. How many fellars? What did they dress like? Which one would I choose?

I whacked my beater and drove the weft into place. I checked that my selvages were still straight and threw my shuttle. It beat all how Lizzie hankered after romance, always singing sad love songs and pestering Aunt Alta to tell the old tales about kings and queens. I could not understand her yearnings. Men! Except Mr. Hill, all they did was spit and chew and make noises from both ends. I was so worn-out listening to her that I decided I might as well have a little fun.

"Oh, they's middlin' fair. About half a dozen, none of them tall as you. Most sort of squatty. Comes from all that tea drinking and eating prissy food. Across the ocean the gentlemen don't grow as tall."

Lizzie's eyes narrowed. "Quit the foolery, Viney. Your mouth doesn't know the taste of truth."

"Me?" My feet marched over the foot pedals. The ropes of the loom creaked on the wooden gears; for me it was like the purring of a cat.

"I heard the Englishmen are asking for eggs and butter. I could cackle, we've eaten so many eggs of late." Lizzie blew back a wayward black curl tickling her cheek. "Thought maybe I'd take this butter over to Delaney Tompkins. Heard the fellars are staying there."

"Oh, Lizzie, leave off on those flatlanders. Marry Lucas. He comes with a pretty cabin and a cow."

"When you come a-visiting me in my fine house in Knoxville, you'll choke on them words." Her little nose went up in the air, and Lizzie thumped the dasher harder.

"Course, I could walk on over with you. I haven't yet seen Sally Tompkins's new babe," I said.

"I don't need no tagalong little sister." Lizzie stuck out her tongue at me.

"If you want to snag one of those gentlemen, you had better mind your book learning. A proper lady says, 'I don't need any little sister tagging along with me.'"

"Then I don't need *any* little sister coming with me, especially you!" She whacked the dasher down so hard, the buttermilk splashed from under the cover of the churn. Lizzie glared at me. "See what you made me do!"

I threw my shuttle and smirked. "Call the dog. He'll lick it up for you."

* * *

The Clear Fork rushed below us as we walked single file along the trail, the scent of damp earth and moldering leaves rising from the trodden path. Pale pink arbutus bloomed in the shelter of outcropping rocks, and patches of white squirrel corn dotted the hillsides. Birds flitted about the woods searching for mates and nesting spots. Lizzie reminded me of one of those little birds with the tufted crest, hopping from tree to tree trying to attract the perfect beau.

I heard the settlers before we reached the Tompkinses'. The thump of axes, the bellowing of oxen, and the shouts of men vibrated through the woods. The Englishmen planned to build on a flat parcel of land that stretched along the ridge. I would have skirted where the men labored, but not Lizzie. She hastened to the edge of the work site and paused.

"Timber!" A big sweet gum crashed across the clearing, and the earth shook.

I went cold and leaned against a chestnut. All the lacy hemlocks and giant oaks had been felled. Sunlight flooded the churned-up forest floor. Sap oozed from stumps protruding like warts across the clearing. Thick boots had trampled trillium, hepaticas, and trout lilies, and piles of logs crushed where the thickest trailing arbutus had thrived. I smelled the bitterness of unearthed goldenseal roots and vowed I'd return and rescue those herbs. This wasn't any little cabin site tucked beneath a cluster of hemlocks with a scrap of a clearing for corn. This was a *town*. I ran into their midst, waving my arms and screaming.

"STOP! You fools!" I yanked the ax from Lucas's hands. "How *could* you?" I swung that ax about me, and the foreigners and neighbors stepped back. The teamsters calmed their wide-eyed oxen.

"Viney!" Lizzie snatched the back of my bodice. "Put that down!"

"You're trespassing, gal," Abel Campbell said. "English bought these four hundred acres from those Yankees."

"They may own it, but you don't have to swing those axes." I searched the faces of my neighbors and foreigners. "Where will you hunt turkeys? Or go wild crafting for ginseng?"

"Paying us cash money to log," Lucas said.

"Just trees. Plenty more." Abel spat. "Lizzie, git your sister out of here. Tell Jacob to take a strap to her."

"He'll do no such thing!" I dug in my heels.

"He should've years ago. Gone! Git! Or I'll switch you myself." Abel stepped toward me shaking his whip.

"Viney!" Lizzie yanked my braid. "Don't shame us more."

I ripped myself from Lizzie's grasp and flung that ax into a stump. *Thud.* Like the Shawnee who once hunted these hills, I declared war on these pasty-faced foreigners! As I turned to go, I noticed one of the men staring at his ax, pondering my words.

"Come on." I said. Once we were out of sight of the men, Lizzie grabbed my shoulders and started shaking me.

"If'n you *ever* humiliate me again that way, I'll . . . slap you! I'm fixing to tell Jacob on you, and Aunt Alta and Aunt Idy . . . and Mrs. Hill!"

"Leave be!" Tears rose inside me. For some queer reason I didn't want Mrs. Hill to know what I'd done. "I had my say." I ran ahead of Lizzie so she'd not see my tears.

By the time we reached Sally's cabin, the sound of chopping had resumed. Sally called to us from the porch, where she was nursing her babe while her other children chased each other.

"Come and sit." The worn wooden rockers on her chair thumped and creaked on the uneven floorboards. I could smell yeast bread rising.

Lizzie pulled off her bonnet. "We brought butter and eggs. Heard the Englishmen were hankering after such."

"You heard right. Mr. Hill will pay for them. Them boys want a hearty spread. Soon as their house is raised, their own cook is coming. Oddest passel of men. They ask for pots of black English tea at all hours of the day. And yeast bread! Most won't eat corn bread."

"Queer lot, for certain," I replied.

"When's the raising?" Lizzie asked.

"Saturday. Two other houses to follow, plus the grand hotel, livery, church, school. Building a regular town, they are. Come June, even bringing in some of their women."

"Blast it!" I muttered. I had to find a way to drive them foreigners off our ridge.

"Do tell," Lizzie crooned. "And do you think they'll be needing any kitchen help in that grand hotel?"

Now isn't that like Lizzie to weasel her way into the goings-on over there? She had probably been pondering this notion ever since we visited the Hills.

"You can ask Mr. Hill. He and a man he calls a geologist rode in yesterday. More men are coming soon. I'm sure they'll be needing help."

Lizzie licked her lips. "Well, I'll just have to speak to Mr. Hill. And this ge-ol-o-gist, what's his name?"

"Lizzie, you don't even know what a geologist is!" I said.

"Hush, Viney!" Lizzie glared at me, and Sally cackled.

"Traitor! How can you even *think* of working for them?"

Lizzie narrowed her eyes. "Sally, I've never been so mortified in all my born days, as by what my little sister did back with those men."

I didn't stay for Lizzie's tale. I took the long route home, climbing down to the river and listening to the current ripple over rocks. A fat hoppytoad rested in a puddle of sun and blinked. By the morrow everyone on the ridge would know what I'd done. Folks already thought me sinfully headstrong, and I reckon I was.

That night I slipped away with a broken hoe blade and a basket. Whip-poor-wills sawed out their names, and bats swooped across the town site. By moonlight the jagged stumps looked like gravestones. Someone sat on the far side of the clearing playing a fiddle.

I ducked down and crawled toward the smell of the goldenseal. My fingers found the crushed stalks and loosened the soil around the plants. I pulled until the roots broke free, and tossed them into my basket. I dug the gnarled ginseng roots and dropped them in, too. What fools these Englishmen were! Destroying the bounty the mountains offered them. They could have transplanted the herbs or harvested them for when they took ill.

But I had to admit, whoever was bowing that fiddle had

clever fingers. I didn't recognize the tune, but his reel was so full of notes, they bounced off each other. I yanked at a ginseng root and grit splattered my face.

"What are you doing?"

Mercy! Sand stung my eyes. Dirt coated my lips. I swiped my sleeve across my mouth. The fiddler ripped through dozens of notes.

"Saving what you fools are destroying." I wiped my eyes with my apron, but I still couldn't see his face. He stepped back into a thread of moonlight. It was the auburn-haired lad who had stared at the Hills and me.

"I didn't know . . . "

"Ain't that the truth!"

"This isn't your land now," he said. Silence swarmed around us.

"Charlie? Who you're talking to?" the fiddler called.

I snatched my basket and dashed toward the woods.

"Wait!" the Englishman shouted. "What are the names of those plants?"

Midway to our cabin I leaned against a beech, feeling the smooth bark on my cheek. If that gent cared enough to know the names of these herbs, why hadn't he tried to save them? And who was that playing fiddle?

Chapter Five

Some of the best instrumental music is of a descriptive
nature, reflecting vividly the incidents of every day life.
Peculiar fingerings of the string, close harmonies . . .
EMMA BELL MILES, *The Spirit of the Mountains*

*n*ext morning Lizzie pulled me from my sleep and insisted we wash every dress, petticoat, and pair of drawers in the cabin.

"But it's Friday!" I protested. "Monday's washday." It seemed Lizzie and I were all tangled. Most days I played the role of the big sister, even though I was younger, but when it came to social doings, Lizzie would stamp her foot and become queen of the cabin.

"Strip the beds, Viney, and start hauling water. I'll light the fire under the kettle," Lizzie commanded.

Eight trips later, steam and the smell of lye soap smarted my eyes as I dumped the last bucket into the rinse tub. Lizzie stoked the fire and sang:

"I wonder when I shall be married,
Oh, be married, be married,

I wonder when I shall be married.
For my beauty's beginning to fade."

I rolled my eyes.

We scrubbed until my knuckles smarted. Lizzie added a heap of starch to our drawers and petticoats, and we spread them over bushes in the sun. She gloated, reckoning we'd have the fullest skirts at the raising. In truth, our drawers would be the scratchiest. Now that we had clean clothes, she demanded that we fill the tub for baths.

"Can't see why," I muttered. "All this fuss for foreigners."

Lizzie splashed and sang. Her singing had a way of softening my spirit, like wakening on an April morning to a bluebird's call. What I could do with my hands, Lizzie created with her voice as she warbled out the words to "Shady Grove." Finally she ordered me in and rubbed the soap across my scalp, making my skin tingle.

"Leave off!" I threw water at Lizzie and ducked down, my hair floating behind me like a mare's tail. I sank to my chin and watched the sunset lick the clouds drifting over the hills.

Jacob had taken his tools and gone early, but Lizzie insisted we arrive after most of the work was over. She was aiming at making an entrance. I looked forward to seeing Mrs. Hill, but I dreaded seeing those heaps of tree stumps.

"Tighter!" Lizzie clung to the door frame as I laced her into the corset Mrs. Hill had given her. "I just have to make me a bustle. Do you reckon Mrs. Hill could find me a pattern?" She craned her neck to look at her plump bottom.

"Why in tarnation do you want a bigger behind? Isn't holding your breath bad enough?" Red flooded her face, and Lizzie looked ready to clobber me.

"You are *impossible*! You don't even have the sense to clean your fingernails!" Lizzie attacked my hair with her tucking comb. "When are you going to start wearing something decent? It's mortifying to be seen with you . . . unlaced and unkempt. At your age, still wearing your hair in a braid! And in front of *gentlemen*. Ain't proper."

"Git!" I grabbed the comb. She'd have yanked every hair out of my head. I braided my hair and tied it with a bit of blue yarn. "If'n we don't hurry a mite, those fellars might take a shine toward the first girls they spy. Not many of them, and lots of us." Lizzie blanched and strode off.

A score of foreigners carried lumber, drove in nails, teasing each other, but I noticed that only a handful of mountain men offered their labors. Later, more highland folk might come for the dancing, but like me, most mourned the mounds of brush and stumps heaped at the edges of the clearing. Lizzie surprised me and walked straight to where the women were arranging food on makeshift tables. After unloading our pies from the baskets, she sidled up to Mrs. Hill.

"Fine afternoon, isn't it, ma'am?" Lizzie gazed up at a sky the shade of wool lifted from an indigo dye pot.

"'Tis lovely. And you look so fresh and fair in that rosy frock. Is that the lace collar you knit this winter?"

"Yes, ma'am. Thank you for teaching me. Only wish I could have bought calico for a new dress instead of having to baste it to this thing."

"You three young folk do tolerably well, but I reckon you don't see much extra cash."

"No, ma'am." Lizzie looked down demurely, but she did not fool me. I knew where this game was headed. Mr. Hill would not refuse Lizzie a job if his wife thought the idea was hers.

Mrs. Hill examined Lizzie. "You are such a tidy young lady. And trustworthy, with an appreciation for fine ways."

"Thank you, ma'am," Lizzie murmured.

"Lizzie, once this boardinghouse is completed, the cook will be needing kitchen help. I wonder if Jacob would give his blessing for you to live here and work? And later the inn will need maids. Mainly you would earn credit at the commissary, but that would help your family."

"Oh, Mrs. Hill! What a generous thought. But I don't know if he and Viney could spare me from the chores."

"You're right about that, Lizzie," I hurried to interject. "I don't know *how* we'd make it without you. Corn and beans need hoeing. Milking, churning, cheese making—tuckers me out just to think on it all."

Lizzie glared at me. Her look could have split kindling.

"Well," Mrs. Hill said. "I'll talk to Jacob and Amos about my idea. Maybe one of the lads apprenticed to us could come to your farm and help now and then."

I grinned while Lizzie stood frozen. Ooo, wouldn't that irk her if I had the company of a foreign fellar all to myself.

"Now, that's a thought, ma'am," I said. "Surely, a young man's hands would be a blessing and could do more work than a girl." I glanced at Lizzie, who looked like she had been sipping vinegar.

"Then I'll speak to the men, and Mr. Hill will inform you when you should come for training." Mrs. Hill patted Lizzie's shoulder.

"Thank you, ma'am," Lizzie said, and marched off to where a few of her girlfriends sat.

"I know it's hard for you to celebrate all this." Mrs. Hill's eyes searched mine. "But trust me, dear, good will come from the settlement."

"Yes, ma'am." But for once, I reckoned Mrs. Hill was wrong. I wondered why I'd even bothered to come to the raising. I wandered over and looked at the oxen staked out to graze. If I had their strength, I'd hitch myself to yonder house and pull it down. But even that would not drive out the English.

At sundown we gathered in the finished boardinghouse. The dining room smelled of fresh-cut pine, and the honey-colored boards glowed in the reflected lantern light. Mr. Tompkins tuned his fiddle while Mr. Lloyd readied his banjo. The black-haired lad I had seen driving the wagon rosined his bow. He must have been the one fiddling when I came rescuing plants.

The eight foreigners stood near Mr. Hill. Lizzie and her girlfriends flounced about the lads, chattering, making them laugh.

"Couple up four!" Mr. Slone called out. The locals nodded to girls and took their hands, but the Englishmen had the strangest ways. A lad with blond hair came up to Lizzie and *bowed*. Made my jaw drop.

I was so busy watching that I jumped when the auburn-haired boy touched my arm. Mercy, did he recognize me?

"Miss, may I have the pleasure of this dance?" he asked. Before I could find my tongue, he grasped my fingers lightly and led me to the center of the room.

"These are country dances?" he asked in his crisp accent as we joined a ring made of two-couple sets. His blue eyes scanned my face.

"Yes." I blushed. I felt like a moth in the lantern light and wondered if he recognized me from that night in the clearing. "We'll dance with Sam and Janie here, and when the caller says to, we'll move on to the next couple. We being the active pair."

"Circle left!" Mr. Slone called. "Now back by the right."

"I see," he murmured in the odd accent.

"Birdie in the cage!" Mr. Slone shouted. "Cage that bird, that pretty little bird!"

I hopped into the center of our foursome, and the others joined hands and circled left around me.

"Birdie hop out and crow hop in!" Sam pushed the foreigner in, and I stepped out.

"Couples move on!" I grabbed the boy's hand, and we slipped on to the next couple.

"Swing that girl across the hall, come back home and swing them all." Tom twirled me and gave me to the foreigner, who turned me with two hands. He was half a foot taller than me.

"Do you have a name?" he asked.

Should I have a little fun or give him the truth? 'Twas a sin to lie.

"Viney Walker." Most times, I liked my name. Puts me in mind of blossoming honeysuckle sweetening the air, with vines strong enough for weaving baskets. But it wasn't one he'd forget.

"Viney?" His frown crinkled the corners of his eyes.

"Short for Lavinia. And you are?"

"Charlie. Charles Breckenridge."

"Duck and Dive," Mr. Slone called.

We bowed under the arching arms of a couple and raised our own arms to sail over the next couple. The foreign fiddler sat on a stool, his boots slapping the floorboards as he drove that tune into our bones. My breathing rose and fell with the beat of the music, and our feet drummed out a rhythm. For a moment we were the heddles and treadles of my loom, weaving a cloth of bodies and music.

"Swing her home!" Mr. Slone barked out.

Charlie placed one hand on my shoulder and another on my waist. "Do the same," he said.

I followed suit, and we swung in a circle like a twirling spindle. Whatever this swinging was called, it surely beat a two-hand turn! When the fiddle stopped, we stood panting.

"Thank you," Charlie said. Once again he grasped my fingertips and guided me away from the center of the room. A group of mountaineers snickered.

"Do you fellars treat all women like royalty?" I bit my tongue when I saw him stiffen. I'd used the same snotty voice he'd heard that night. Might as well have called out: "I'm the one!"

"And did the plants survive the transplanting? I would like to learn which ones you took."

He *had* recognized me! My face reddened. "Goldenseal and ginseng," I mumbled, then threaded my way through a cluster of couples and slipped out into the dark, once again fleeing from that foreigner.

CHAPTER SIX

. . . and in the dusk [we] saw the bright gleam of light under the verandahs of two sightly wooden houses . . . In one of these, the temporary restaurant, we were seated in a few minutes at an excellent tea.

THOMAS HUGHES

"Turncoat. Judas. How can you work for the foreigners?" I ran out of words for traitor. Whirling my quilling wheel, I filled more bobbins for my shuttle. "You don't have to live there. Could walk back and forth."

"Ain't walking such a far piece every day. 'Sides, I *want* to live in town," Lizzie said as she filled a basket with her dresses. "Just bettering myself as I best know how."

"If you really cared about bettering yourself, you'd read the Hills' books. Improve your grammar."

"Folks say you read too much! Say all those books addled your brain. Say it ain't natural for a sixteen-year-old gal not to be wanting a man and young'uns."

"Well, you aren't wed!"

"But folks don't gossip about me. Enough fellars brushed my lips to know I enjoy men."

"I'm sure they have." I watched Lizzie march off toward the settlement.

Without Lizzie, I had to tend to everything: cheese making, washing, ironing, cleaning, and hoeing the garden, and the corn, and milking Cindy Lou. Dust sifted onto the crossbeam of my loom; I felt snarled inside and missed Lizzie's singing to lighten the work. I hummed, but it wasn't the same. Lizzie and I were like honey and yeast—without sweetening, the yeast wouldn't rise as high.

"Can't keep on like this." I tossed the dishwashing water on my rosebush. "Need to ask for help. Mrs. Hill said they'd send over a gent."

"I'm not lief to be beholding to some foreigner." Jacob squinted at the needle he was attempting to thread. The worn harness sprawled at his feet like a small dog.

"I'm a-mind to stop hoeing. I promised Barbara Rae I'd finish her coverlet by Independence Day. If'n you don't send for help, those weeds'll smother the corn." I rolled down my sleeves against the chilling night air.

Jacob grunted and handed me his needle. I slipped the linen thread through the needle's eye and slicked it with a lump of beeswax. Holding the needle behind my back, I raised my eyebrows.

"Well?" I inched my toes along the floorboards, feeling the cracks. "Can't tell how many needles I've lost to these cracks. Seems they always fall through when I drop them."

"Viney." Weariness oozed from Jacob's lips. Even at nineteen, grubbing sprouts all day took the starch out of him.

"Here." I picked up the harness. "My hands are strong enough. Let me help."

"I'll speak to Amos." Jacob slumped back in the chair, closing his eyes.

About a week later, I sat on a porch step sharpening my hoe. Fog licked the grass in the field where Cindy Lou grazed, and dew clung to the cupped rose petals scenting the air. Mrs. Hill had once told me that this rose set her in mind of one she saw winding up a castle tower in England. She thought it queer to find it here, along with the bushes she calls boxwood, but I reckon my kin brought the plants from across the ocean. I breathed in the freshness of the morning, knowing that the summer sun would soon wipe it away.

Suddenly, the guinea fowl set to screaming. One of the gray hens shrieked and lit into an Englishman. She beat his chest with her wings, knocking his hat off.

"Great Heavens!" Charlie shouted. He waved his arms and dashed toward me.

It was wrong, but I waited a mite before saving the lad. I relished having the upper hand. "Go on! Git!" I slapped my apron at the guineas pecking Charlie's legs. Picking up my hoe, I swung it, careful-like. They scattered, screeching and flapping, into the sassafras. I picked up Charlie's hat, and with the blade of my hoe scraped hen poop off the brim. He was breathing hard, and the blue of his eyes looked like the center of a flame.

"Thank you, Miss Lavinia." Charlie accepted his hat. "Do all mountain folk keep fowl that attack?"

I shrugged. "Most have hounds. Some meet you with a gun. I like birds."

"Ah, I see. Mr. Hill sent me to help with your hoeing." Charlie bowed slightly. "At your service, miss."

"Where's your hoe?" I didn't recall seeing him drop it during the ruckus. I held up mine. "One hoe. You fellars name it something different in your land?"

"Nooo . . . " His neck turned red.

"You come to work without?" I blurted out. What sort of twitter-witted fool did Mr. Hill send us?

"I leaned it against the Hills' barn and walked away . . . Perhaps . . . may I borrow one, please?"

"Here. Take mine. I'll fetch Lizzie's." Charlie's eyes glinted when I said her name. Tarnation, that gal was as swift as an adder in striking men. "Jacob's over yonder. Slip through the sassafras."

Lizzie's hoe was duller than a toad, so by the time I sharpened it and reached the field, Charlie and Jacob were working their rows. I picked up about four rows over from Charlie. I whacked at the lamb's-quarter, always tough to unearth, and minced the purslane. Charlie stopped, pulled up some quack grass, and sliced a pumpkin with his hoe.

"Heh! Can't you tell a pumpkin from a weed?" I marched over. Didn't this boy know *anything*?

"I thought you said that corn grew here." He fingered the scratchy leaves.

"Yes, and runner beans, squash, and pumpkins," I said, pointing out each plant. "The beans climb the cornstalks; the others crawl about. Smother the weeds and their itchy leaves keeps the coons out of the corn."

"Clever. Very clever to plant them together so that the squash and pumpkins guard the corn from the raccoons."

"We're not dim-witted." I walked away and set to hoeing. "Arrogant fool," I muttered.

By midmorning Charlie was eight rows behind me. He would pause and inspect his hands. I had a blister rising on the side of my thumb, so I suspected that his hands were raw. He twisted his neck and shoulders like they ached, too. Jacob had reached the far end of the field. I finished my piece and started in on Charlie's rows, moving back toward him.

"You needn't hoe my rows. I'm here to assist you." Charlie dragged his sleeve across his forehead.

I snorted. "What you don't finish, we'll do sooner or later."

"There's always tomorrow." His hoe jerked in and out of the overlapping leaves.

"Is that so?" I didn't mean to sound so sassy, but I figured those blisters would hold him back from hoeing for several days.

"I *want* to be a farmer." His shoulders stiffened. Mercy, he was a touchy one. A body had to mind every word around this fellar.

"Then you need to learn *how* to hoe. Need to find that rhythm. You're a dandy swinger. If'n your shoulders and body move with the hoe, it won't tire you so."

Charlie's mouth cracked, showing a chipped tooth. "I am astounded that you perceive me capable of anything!"

I tied my tongue as Jacob came alongside us and scowled at me. He and Charlie gabbed about the colony. Appeared that Charlie was a year younger than Jacob, and he pestered my brother with questions about farming. Long about noon, we stood at the end of the rows. I could tell that Jacob took a shine to Charlie.

"Thank ye. Come visit us sometime." Jacob shook Charlie's hand, and he winced.

"My pleasure." Charlie extended his hand to me.

"If'n you want to use those hands tomorrow, best allow me to bandage them." I nodded my head at the cabin. "There's wash water on the porch."

Charlie gritted his teeth while I rubbed my red oil into his palms and wrapped them with clean muslin. I followed his eyes and saw that he was examining our climbing rose.

"My mother raises such a plant. She calls it a Grenville, one of the *Rosa multiflora*."

"Well, folks here call it the Seven Sisters."

"What's this brew?" Charlie nodded at my tin of red oil.

"Lousewort. Weeds."

"Can you identify the plants growing in this terrain?"

I stared at him. "I've traipsed all over this ridge, and Aunt Alta taught me most of the plants' names. And trees." I tucked the end of the muslin into the bandage, encasing his palm.

"Will you teach me about the flora?" His gentian blue eyes scanned the sky to the west.

I followed his gaze and watched mare's tail clouds spread like a fleece over the mountains. Was God pulling His cards, fanning out the thin clouds like I carded wool?

"*Cirrus*," Charlie muttered.

"What?"

"*Cirrus* is the Latin name for that wispy type of cloud."

"Clouds have Latin names?"

"Yes. Just like this *Rosa multiflora*." Charlie nodded his head toward the blooming Seven Sisters.

"All I know is, it's fixing to rain when mare's tails ride the sky. Hear that robin? He's singing his rain song, too."

"Really?" Charlie leaned over the porch railing. "And you call those clouds mare's tails? I must note that name in my weather journal—a daily account I keep of my scientific observations. Teach me your plants' names, and I'll teach you the Latin names for clouds." Charlie turned around and smiled.

"Might." I liked the way his mouth curved, and a wisp of an idea floated across my mind.

Chapter Seven

Those who should not go are: the man who never mends things, because he cannot drive a nail without pounding his fingers, and then blaming the hammer.

THOMAS HUGHES

Soon the runner beans climbed the corn and the squash plants crept across the field. Charlie trudged up our path about once a week during June. Most hours he labored with Jacob while I worked about the cabin or in the garden. Precious little time to study the trees and clouds, but in a spare moment I'd tell Charlie about the plants that grew nearby. The day Charlie came to clean the barn, the fiddler joined him.

"May I introduce Seamus O'Donnell," Charlie said. "From Boston."

"Please to meet you." Seamus extended the hand that was so quick with the bow. His home might have been Boston, but the lilt in his voice softened his words.

"But you don't talk like a Yankee, nor like the English." I shook his hand.

"God forbid! My da and mum left Ireland during the Great Hunger. From County Mayo. Surely I sound like them."

"Morning," Jacob called from the barn. "Best begin before the heat rises." He nodded toward the sun topping the crest of the trees.

I settled in to my churning on the porch as the lads filled the wagon with manure. Their sweaty shirts clung to their backs, and the stench of dung drifted to the porch. Even my mother's roses could not freshen the air. I'd have gone inside, but the cabin was stuffy. I chewed on mint leaves, ruminating. Why *did* these foreigners come here? Why not buy a farm in Ireland or England? Why had Seamus said, "God forbid"? I watched the woolly clouds send long shadows that crept like cats over the hills. I'd finished rinsing and salting the butter when boots clattered up the steps. I dashed to the door and latched it.

"We're parched!" Jacob hollered. "Open up." He rattled the door.

"You all can hightail it to the spring. I'm not cleaning up after you." One set of muck-covered boots was trouble enough, but I'd not allow three pairs to dirty my clean floor.

By the time the lads appeared with slicked-back hair, I had mugs of cool mint tea set out on the porch. They drank up while I wrapped my butter in wet muslin and packed it in a basket, adding a crock of curds just to show Lizzie that I could make cheese without her.

"Off to see Lizzie?" Jacob asked me. I noticed Charlie stopped swallowing for a second, but Seamus kept drinking.

"Yes." I slapped more wet leaves around the butter for cooling. I wouldn't let on that I missed my sister, especially at night when we would whisper about our futures or gossip about friends. Most times, Jacob felt like a pa to me.

"May we escort you to the settlement?" Charlie asked.

"Suppose so." I had hoped Charlie would be walking that way. Like plying two strands of yarn together, I had mulled over the idea that being seen with Charlie might hush talk about me staying single. I hadn't counted on Seamus's company, but strolling with two gents might convince folks that I was finally becoming like other girls. But I'd be careful and not appear too friendly.

"May I carry your basket?" Charlie offered. "Then you could point out the different woodland plants. Where did you plant the ones you stole?"

"I didn't steal. I rescued them." I wanted to spit out more, but I knew that courting girls had to mind their manners and humor the man.

Charlie's face flamed. "Miss Viney, I would prefer not to argue, but rather to learn from you."

His sincere words squished me like an ant beneath his feet.

Seamus strolled up and eyed us. "Begging your pardon, miss, but you know Charlie's English. Cocky lot. Could you be so kind as to name us the plants?" Even his speech rippled like a fiddle tune.

Charlie frowned at Seamus. Was he a bit jealous of Seamus's charm?

"Here." I smiled at Charlie and threaded my way through the mayapples. "That's goldenseal, with a maple-shaped leaf. Has a little white flower in the spring. The roots are good for fevers." I pointed at a five-leafed plant. "Ginseng.

Folks off the mountain pay cash money for the roots. I dig it in the fall, but I always leave some plants so as to keep the patch growing. And dandelion roots are good for the liver."

"*Cumulus*," Charlie pointed toward the hills. "Cumulus clouds forecast fair weather. But when they mound up and level off in an anvil shape, a storm is gathering."

Well, any fool knows that! I bit my tongue. "*Cumulus* is another Latin word?"

"Yes, scientists always use Latin when identifying natural objects. They probably have Latin names for most of these plants."

"Can you speak Latin?" I had always wanted to learn Latin or French. Riled me when I read Mr. Hill's book to find words in those tongues and not know their meanings.

"Well." Charlie picked a twig off a spicebush and snapped it. "I earned better marks in the natural sciences."

Seamus began to chant:

"Latin is a dead tongue
As dead as dead can be.
First it killed the Romans,
And now it's killing me!"

He cuffed Charlie on the shoulder.

"And *that's* why I want to farm." Charlie yanked off Seamus's hat and dashed down the trail. Seamus tackled him, and they fell to the ground. The two of them put me in mind of puppies tussling, not eighteen-year-old men ready to start a farm. Charlie trotted up next to me.

"What's that tree?" he asked.

"Sweet gum. See the star-shaped leaves?" Far off from the settlement, I heard pounding like a hundred horses' hooves on frozen ground. My heart beat faster as the hammering grew louder. We walked from the shade of the forest into a milling mess.

The glare of the sun stabbed my eyes as the rays struck stacks of lumber and glinted on the dozens of hammers. Men scrambled up ladders and eased across roof rafters while others sawed lumber. Beams and boards towered upward, forming the shell of a monster. Five more gleaming buildings bordered a road with heat waves rising off it.

How many trees had they butchered for this? How many more would perish? Where would the thrush nest? And what happened to the wildflowers? I wanted to flee.

I hated the foreigners. A plague on them all. Tears prickled my eyelids. "Just tell me where Lizzie is. Point the way."

"She works in the boardinghouse," Seamus answered. "We should escort you."

Charlie reached out to take my arm, but I wouldn't let him see my tears. I dashed away, dodging the wagons rumbling about us. Men cursed my flapping skirts as the mules balked. The air was thick with sawdust and sweat. My feet pounded up the board steps. I flung open the door.

Lizzie's behind stuck out like a beaver dam. Head cocked, she smiled up at the yellow-haired gent who had asked her to dance. He was fastening a locket about her slim throat and looked like he was aiming to kiss her.

"Git your hands off of her!" I swung my basket and aimed all my fury at the Englishman. He backed away, scowling.

"Viney!" Lizzie yanked me away. "Leave George alone!" Her fingernails dug into my shoulder.

"Blasted Englishman. Messing with my sister." I tried to twist free.

Lizzie's hand met my cheek, and the slap burned to my toes. I reeled back, sucking in air, willing myself not to cry.

"And who is this guttersnipe?" George fussed with his waistcoat.

"My *little* sister who thinks she owns this ridge, and me."

"Sister?" George's eyes inched over me. "How could *you* be related to this ragged urchin?"

I waited for Lizzie to defend me, but she curled her fingers over George's forearm.

"Viney's a bossy, willful *child*. Please forgive her." Lizzie stood on tiptoe and kissed his cheek. "I'll see to her."

"Tea at five." George chucked her under the chin and walked out the door.

Lizzie's words knocked the fight out of me. She grabbed my arm, dragged me into the kitchen, and slammed the door.

"Don't you ever shame me again," she hissed. The silver locket rose and fell like a star against her tight bodice. "If'n you can't behave like a lady, then keep to the cabin. Comin' into town dressed like trash!"

"Who you calling names? You fool with that gentleman, and he'll use you. Leave you for trash. That kind isn't looking for a wife. See how they destroyed the land! And why isn't King George out hammering nails like those other fellows?

Charlie and Seamus said Mr. Hill needed every man to help build."

Lizzie smirked. "George only works three mornings a week. He came over with money. Being late afternoon, the gentlemen of quality come in to dress for tea. Charlie and that Irish boy are apprenticed out."

"Least they're learning how to work." My cheek prickled with fire. Lizzie might have pinched me or pulled my hair, but she'd never struck me. And to hit me in front of that foreigner!

She tugged on her cuffs and smoothed her apron. Her new purple calico dress sprigged with gold leaves shimmered like the petals on Mrs. Hill's irises. Rows of buttons marched up her new black boots. Who had paid for this finery? The door between rooms opened, and an older woman wearing a frilly white cap entered.

"What's amiss, Lizzie? I heard shouting." The woman spoke with an English accent.

Lizzie dipped a little curtsy. "My sister Viney doesn't know her place, Mrs. Johnstone. She was rude to a gentleman."

Mrs. Johnstone surveyed me, pursing her lips and standing up even straighter. I reckon she didn't like my homespun and bare feet. And that I wore no bonnet.

"Next time, use the back door. The one for servants."

The words that flamed inside me should not be said by a Christian girl, so I clenched my jaw until my teeth ached. Didn't know my place, huh? Oh, but I did. I'd never rub against some gent's shoulder and murmur in his ear just to squeeze money from his pockets. I dumped the butter and cheese on the trestle table.

"I *do* know my place. It's at my loom. I'll be no man's play-pretty!" I shoved open the "servant's door" and headed home.

CHAPTER EIGHT

Those who should not go are: he who thinks the world owes him a living . . . without hard work.

THOMAS HUGHES

Boots thumped up the steps and knuckles rapped on the door. "Viney?" Mr. Hill called. I hadn't seen him or the lads for a month.

"Come in. Sit a spell." I whacked the beater twice and let go.

"Thank you, but no time for sitting. Mrs. Hill broke her arm last night."

"Mercy! How can I help?"

"If you could come over. Stay a few weeks, we'd be obliged."

"You spoke with Jacob?"

"Yes. He understands. I could bring your wheel along."

"Thank you." I set to packing.

Mr. Hill lifted the great wheel from its frame and carried it to his wagon. I hated leaving my loom, but Mrs. Hill had treated Lizzie and me like kin. I wanted to repay her kindness and living nearer Charlie would be handy for my plan. Ridge folks would notice and talk.

Dirty dishes lined the Hills' table when I marched into the kitchen. I peeked at Mrs. Hill. She slept with her long gray braids snaked across the quilt. A bouquet of honeysuckle stood on the dresser and scented the room.

I heated water, shaved soap, and lit into the dishes, sweat rolling down my back. Through a window I watched several young roosters scratching about the barnyard. Mrs. Hill would be kicking apart a cockfight if she didn't stew up a few of those birds. After these dishes, I would do in one myself.

I inched across the clearing, holding my apron wide, and slowly guided four of the cocks toward the open barn door. They kept looking about, ready to bolt, but they figured the barn would be safe. One smarter bird squawked and leapt over my shoulder, flying up into an oak. I edged the three remaining birds into a dark corner, and they crashed into each other, squallering. Keeping clear of their spurs, my hands darted low and grabbed one.

I don't relish butchering and cleaning chickens, especially in such heat, but I kept thinking about how chicken soup would be good for Mrs. Hill. I was holding my breath against the stench of scalded feathers when I heard a ruckus out in the peach orchard. I dropped the bird and ran toward the shouting. Had someone fallen from a ladder?

Baskets of peaches surrounded Charlie and Seamus, and the Hills' team stood quietly in the shade, their tails flicking away flies. But King George and another Englishman, plus two young ladies wearing straw hats, had reined in their horses near the orchard.

"Be good lads, and fill our hats with peaches," the lanky youth ordered. "Make haste."

The surliness in his English voice reminded me of all that I hated about these arrogant invaders. Why weren't these two helping with the building or farming? Isn't that why they came? I itched to stuff a peach down his gullet. Sliding between the trees, I rolled a hard peach between my fingers. Peach fuzz drifted from the branches and prickled my neck.

"Pick them yourselves," Charlie answered, and kept filling his basket.

"Not you, Breckenridge. The Paddy. Quick, boy, the sun's beastly hot."

"Shady under these trees," Seamus called, and set a basket on the wagon.

"Of all the cheek." His Majesty jumped from his horse. "I'll teach you how to address a gentleman."

"Robert, leave off. We'll be late for tea," George called.

I pitched that peach, and it walloped Robert on the shoulder. He staggered back. Charlie threw a rotten peach that splattered across Robert's shirt. Seamus aimed a juicy one and struck George in the stomach. Tickled me to see how red those Englishmen turned.

The ladies squealed. Horses reared. The gents cursed as peaches flew. Robert jumped into his saddle and shook his whip.

"Just you wait!" he roared, and they galloped toward the settlement.

I set out hot water when the lads came in for supper. They stripped out of their fuzzy shirts and soaped up while I ladled chicken and dumplings into their bowls. Mrs. Hill sat at the table with her arm resting on a pillow.

"You're a saint, Viney," Mrs. Hill said after saying the blessing. She sipped a spoonful of broth.

"Aye, and a grand cook." Seamus stuffed half a dumpling in his mouth.

"What was all the commotion?" Mrs. Hill asked. "Sounded like frightened horses."

"Gents riding by, mum." Charlie answered. "Their horses spooked."

It wasn't a complete lie, but I spied Charlie's foot nudging Seamus's. I concentrated on slicing my dumpling into tiny bites. Had they figured out who had thrown that first peach?

After supper the lads retreated to the porch, but I overheard their whispers as they laced up their boots.

"But if you didn't throw that first peach, then who did?" Charlie asked.

"Only one other pair of feet trod this farm," Seamus replied. "Quick, little feet."

"Viney?" Charlie stretched and rubbed his shoulder. "Why would she defend us?"

"Did I hear a body say my name?" I stepped out and eased the screen door back into place.

Seamus grinned. "You've a powerful arm. Good aim."

"Thank you. Comes from hauling water. Who was that boy ordering you about? Royalty?"

"No, just another Englishman who thinks he owns the world." Seamus tightened his bootlaces. "An Englishman with plenty of silver in his pockets."

"But your family came from across the sea."

"He's Irish," Charlie answered, as if that explained everything.

"And hardworking and a fine fiddler," I added.

"I'm no more than a clod of dirt to Robert," Seamus said. "Someone to order about. English don't mingle with the Irish."

"But what's Charlie, then? You two frolic like brothers."

"Charlie's different." Seamus nudged Charlie. "He has the soul of an Irishman."

Red crept up Charlie's neck, and he stood up quickly. "Thank you for the splendid repast, Miss Viney." He bowed slightly and climbed onto the wagon seat. Seamus winked at me and hopped on, too.

I flopped into a rocker and watched a cloud of dust engulf the wagon loaded with peaches. Those two puzzled me. Or was it just Charlie? He came from England, but he didn't act like Robert. Why did Charlie destroy ginseng for a house and then pester me to name him the plants? Made no sense at all.

Later that night I heard Seamus's fiddling from out in the wood where the lads camped. Crawling to the end of my bed, I closed my eyes and listened to the slow, sad notes of his tune flowing like sorghum molasses off a spoon. Was this a song like the mournful ballads Lizzie sang? Or did the Irish dance to such sorrowful music? I wound the tune inside my head to remember when I gazed at the tree stumps stacked along the edges of the settlement.

Chapter Nine

They (the older women) are the nurses, the teachers of practical arts, the priestesses and their wisdom commands respect of all.

Emma Bell Miles, *The Spirit of the Mountains*

I'd been home nigh a month when Lizzie sashayed up the porch steps. I was shucking dry beans for the winter, a chore she and I had shared. We had made a contest out of it, racing to see who could shuck the most, the fastest.

"You must come. There's so much to do before the grand opening." Lizzie swung her sunbonnet by a tie while our calico cat rubbed her ankles.

"Apples to dry. Need to sew Jacob some new shirts. Loom sits idle. Why should I help the foreigners?"

Lizzie leaned over and petted the cat. "Sorry about that afternoon." She glanced up at me. "I was . . . a bit hasty."

Hearing Lizzie's apology felt like chewing honeycomb. Reckon, despite our differences, we were both muleheaded Walkers.

"Also, Mrs. Hill sent me. Said she'd be obliged if you'd help with the sewing. Curtains, pillows, and such. Said she'd needed you fierce. Said she'd never finish on time without you."

I smiled, pleased to think Mrs. Hill thought so highly of me.

Lizzie brushed cat hair from her hem. Tiny black roses danced across her dress of Turkey red calico. I wish I could find some of that red dye supposed to make the most lasting of colors. The rich calico brought snap to Lizzie's eyes and a rosy tint to her cheeks. George's silver locket shattered the sunlight. For a moment I felt like an acorn plopped beneath a mountain laurel creamy with blossoms.

"Are those snotty rich boys roughing up their hands yet?"

"Yes." Lizzie glowered at me. "Mr. Hughes arrived early this month. At first light he was up supervising the planting and painting."

"What's he like?" I dropped a handful of maroon and white beans into a bowl.

"If'n you want to know, come see for yourself." Lizzie tied on her bonnet, forming a bow to one side of her chin. Her boots clattered down the stairs, and like a setting sun, she slipped between the trees.

I'd pulled the worst of the weeds and finished the mending before I trudged off toward the settlement. A few red leaves flickered among the sassafras trees, purple asters bloomed at the end of our clearing, and crumpled ferns crunched beneath my bare feet. 'Twas almost a year since I first spied the foreigners. I tallied all they'd taken from me: acres of trees and wildflowers, flocks of songbirds, and my own sister, calling me names and slapping me. How much more would I lose? The scream of the sawmill sliced the forest as I approached the settlement. I hated that machine.

I scowled at the gleaming monstrosity towering close to the treetops. Men stood on scaffolding, painting the clapboards white. Above the three stories other gents nailed shake shingles to the roof boards. A veranda wrapped about the inn, and in the middle of its roof, a small room jutted over the porch like a big eye.

I'd given up climbing trees when Jacob, Lizzie, and I moved into our own cabin. Just too busy hoeing and keeping house. But seeing that half-pint room, I felt that dizzy yearning to climb a tree and look over the wrinkles of the ridge. By nightfall I planned to stand in that room.

Teams hitched to wagons loaded with barrels and crates waited by the veranda. I dodged the men grading a road. I felt my ire bubbling like corn mash. The best wild strawberry patch on the ridge had grown beneath that road. I scanned the edges of the gravel for plants that might have escaped the grader but only saw a few brown leaves and twisted, dry roots.

Near the servants' door I bumped into Seamus carrying two buckets. Plaster dust blotched his face, making him look like a leper.

"Morning, Miss Viney. Come to assist your sister?" He nodded his head and dust sifted from his curls.

"Morning. Mrs. Hill asked for me." I grabbed the door, and Lizzie looked up from a basin of sudsy water and dishes.

"Finally! I reckoned you'd never come. Only a week left before the grand opening." She dried her hands on her apron. "I'm ruining my hands washing dishes. Be a lamb and finish."

"Spinning would soften them again. Thought I was called to sew."

"Mrs. Hill is still eating breakfast with Mr. Hughes. You can have them dishes clean by the time they drink their last cup of tea." She glanced at my hands. "Besides, washing will clean your fingers. Wouldn't do to stain them fancy woven goods Mr. Hughes fetched on."

I rolled up my sleeves. What would English weaving look like?

She glanced at my bare feet. "Will you ever learn to dress decently? I could lend you my old boots."

"No thank you. My feet are wider. And if you want my help, you shut that mouth."

I scrubbed egg off a gold-rimmed china plate, wondering why I'd allowed Lizzie to talk me into doing her work. I glanced about the kitchen. Huge copper pots hung over a cookstove, and cast-iron skillets dangled from an overhead beam. More china sparkled on shelves that lined the walls. I could smell yeast bread rising in a twelve-quart crockery bowl. A door swung open, and Janie Slone smiled at me.

"Viney! I never thought to see you here." Janie set down a tray with dirty teacups. Mrs. Hill followed her.

"So good of you to come, lass. Did you bring your thimble? The best light is in the parlor," said Mrs. Hill, leading the way. Her buttoned boots clicked like chinquapins falling on a tin roof, but my bare feet slid silently on the polished floor. I could see my reflection in the shine of the boards, and more dark woodwork rose halfway up the white walls.

Mrs. Hill opened a massive door, and I gasped. Mounds of fabric, inky black, maroon, and dark green, glowed from the table. I ran my fingers over the shimmering brocades. My pulse quickened.

"How do they weave such cloth, ma'am? What makes these colors?" If Mrs. Hill hadn't been with me, I would have kissed the brocade.

"Special looms in England are used to create such complex patterns, and they use new chemical dyes for those colors." Mrs. Hill cocked her head. "I appreciate you coming, Viney. I know your distaste for the settlement, but please believe me, Mr. Hughes is a good man. For years he labored for better working conditions for weavers in the English mills."

"Yes, ma'am." I drew my thimble from my apron pocket. "Where should I begin?"

"Please hem these curtains. They're already pinned. I can't promise you cash money for your labors, but you can take your wages in trade at the commissary once the building is finished."

"Thank you, ma'am." I pulled a chair next to a window, and Mrs. Hill picked up her sewing.

Only a few minutes after we commenced sewing, a tall man strode into the room, with hair that glowed like a ripe persimmon. He dressed, like Charlie, in a flannel shirt and corduroy britches and galluses, and his blue eyes studied me.

"Good morning, ladies. And would you be the talented Miss Walker? I am Thomas Hughes." Mr. Hughes gave me his hand.

"Please to meet you, sir. I'm Viney to all on the ridge." His grip was firm, but his hands were soft. Appeared Mr. Hughes talked about work more than performing it.

"Mrs. Hill showed me your coverlet. Beautiful work. How do you spin so finely?"

"Aunt Alta taught me, sir. Can't recollect a time when I wasn't spinning."

"And those dyes! Browns and golds like these autumn leaves. What did you use?"

"Walnuts. Goldenrod, sir." Mr. Hughes words slid through me like molasses taffy. Folks on the ridge wanted my coverlets but seldom praised.

"And Mrs. Hill said you created your own designs! Who taught you such artistry?"

"Reckon the Lord gave me that gift, sir. I study the light through the tree leaves, or the way the bark circles a knot on a limb, and work the patterns into my weaving." Queer how this fellar's eyes never left mine. Wondered if he noticed I wasn't wearing boots?

"Do you have two coverlets that I might purchase?"

"Why . . . I reckon so, sir. I've a couple woven with walnut and cream. Would they suit you?"

"Splendid! Please bring them tomorrow. I'll take one back to England with me, and the other will grace a room of this inn. We'd like to display a few mountain crafts for our guests." Mr. Hughes bowed slightly and marched toward the stairs.

"Yes, sir. Thank you, sir." I felt like a fish flopping on a riverbank gasping for air. I had never dreamed that one of my weavings would sail across the sea. I felt as if I was sending one of my children to that foreign land. Why had I said yes without thinking?

"How wonderful." Mrs. Hill squeezed my shoulder. "I'm so proud of you."

Her words warmed me like milk and honey on a frosty night.

All day my mind chased that moment, like a kitten racing after a ball of yarn. When the light dimmed, I folded my sewing. Time to search for that little room.

Most of the workers had washed and stacked their tools. Probably off drinking tea in pressed linen shirts. I took the steps two at a time. Door after door marched down the narrow hallways. I paused at the third floor, calculating which hall held that room. Faint voices skipped across the polished floor. I followed them, recognizing Lizzie's coo.

"You are such a dear. Could you please tie the ribbon for me?"

My stomach sank. George again. Why did he have to drag Lizzie up here? I halted in the doorway.

Silhouetted against the window light, Charlie slipped his hands under Lizzie's curls and fumbled with a ribbon. Lizzie's bustle brushed his knees. I wanted to shake Lizzie; her endless flirting would spoil my plan! What did she want with a boy yearning to farm? Footsteps sounded behind me.

"Come for the view?" Seamus asked. At the sound of his voice, Lizzie whirled around and shot me a calculated look.

"And what brings y'all way up here?" she asked.

"The sunset. I aimed to see it above the treetops." I noticed Lizzie squeeze Charlie's hand. "Thought George spent his evenings with you?"

"Mercy, I forgot. Mrs. Hill asked for extra candles in the ladies' parlor." Lizzie's skirt swooshed across the floor.

"Grand clouds, aren't they? The color of ripe peaches." Seamus leaned against the window trim. "Cumulus or cirrus?"

Charlie roused himself like a duck rising from the bottom of the river. "Peaches?" he muttered.

I had no claim to this lad, but for some queer reason it riled me so see him fall to Lizzie's charms.

Chapter Ten

That's Pineburr, a mighty sweet draft. By now I know
it so well that I can weave it right on without
even flashin' my eye on the paper.
F R A N C E S   G O O D R I C H ,   *Mountain Homespun*

The morning before the grand opening, the mountains ripped apart the low clouds, and rain sheeted across the ridge. I awoke on a pallet in Janie Slone's room and stared at the plastered ceiling. I had to admit that plaster and paint brightened a room, made it easier to sew after dark. When Janie stirred, I pestered her with questions about Lizzie and George, and Charlie.

"I think Charlie's catching on to Lizzie. And George's like the other rich gents," Janie said. "After whatever he can get. Lizzie's met her match in him."

"Have to think of a way to make those gents want to leave."

"Don't see how you'll manage that." Janie pinned up her hair. "And would you want to be shut of Seamus and Charlie, too?"

"No. . . . What are folks saying about them? About me?"

"Tickled to see you with them. Comparing you to Lizzie, baiting several hooks."

Appeared my scheme was working, but perhaps too well. I didn't have a peace about folks thinking I was becoming like Lizzie.

"If'n you want breakfast, best hurry." Janie tied on her apron.

"Whose the turncoat now?" Lizzie asked as I bit into a biscuit. "Weaving for the foreigners. Spending the night."

"Only because Mrs. Hill and I sewed until late. I'd never want to live here. Too many men cussing and spitting. And Janie said George's the sort that messes with girls. You be careful."

"I know what I'm doing. Do you?" Lizzie picked up a tray holding covered dishes. The scent of scrambled eggs and grits seeped between the lids. "Mighty friendly with those two lads."

Red rose up my neck. "They're honorable lads. Hardworking, too."

"Is that so? George and Robert are gentlemen, too," Lizzie said. "Even volunteered to fetch in the fine folks coming on the train. So I don't want to hear anymore about them being lazy." She marched through the door to the dining room.

King George and Royal Robert? They'd do anything to avoid hard work.

On the veranda I saw Jacob and Lucas ripping boards off huge wooden boxes that held furniture. Mr. Hill had promised extra credit at the commissary to the locals who hired on for the day. Other fellars trudged through the halls carrying chairs and bed parts, and leaving muddy footprints. Such mud would slow the wagons and tire the horses fetching in the foreigners. Couldn't have thought of a better way to plague this grand opening. Charlie and Seamus lumbered down the staircase toward us.

"Good morning, Miss Viney," Charlie said.

"Pleasant morning." Seamus winked at me. "Irish weather, is it not?"

"Reckon. And what do you call these clouds?" I asked Charlie. "Any predictions for the morrow?" Charlie needed a haircut. But I rather liked the way his hair bounced around his collar, put me in mind of when he swung me.

"*Stratus*, Latin for layers," Charlie said. "And the needle on my aneroid barometer fell to twenty-nine point six. Means more storms are coming."

"Your *what*?"

"A barometer is a tool that forecasts the weather. It's with my gear in the barn."

"Come on," Seamus said, and pulled Charlie toward a pile of furniture.

Other girls from the ridge flitted about carrying bundles of linens. I climbed the polished oak stairs. The railing came from a famous English inn where a man named Chaucer wrote a book of tales hundreds of years ago. Odd to think of a scrap of wood boated over to the Cumberland Mountains.

"Viney!" Mrs. Hill called from across the hall. She stood in the room with my coverlet draped on a bed built by Lucas. One of my rag rugs brightened the floor, and a splint-bottom chair woven by Jacob rested in a corner.

"Doesn't it look splendid? You bring honor to this ridge."

Mrs. Hill's praise bubbled through me like hard cider. Oh, how I relished her smile. For a moment I pretended she was my mama admiring the work of my hands.

"Do you have any scraps that you could sew into pillows?" Mrs. Hill asked. "I know there is not much time, but this morning I realized that pillows would add to the decor. And perhaps a piece of weaving for a small lap rug?"

"I reckon I could sew a few pillows, ma'am." I fancied the way the swirl of the Pine Burr pattern matched the curly maple headboard of the bed. "Have to go fetch the weavings."

"Oh dear, in all this wet. Maybe Jacob would lend you his mule?"

"Yes, ma'am."

I ran to the stables, where King George stood under an overhang while Seamus led out a second team. Royal Robert sat on his wagon seat clutching the reins to his horses. Rain ran down the gents' oilskins, and tarps covered the back of the wagons.

"Look sharp," Robert called. He rattled off, spraying mud over Seamus.

Arrogant Englishman to the core. I hated Robert. Thinking he owned everyone and everything. Never a please or thank-you from his lips.

King George climbed onto his wagon and rumbled away. Seamus dragged his shirt across his face, and I walked into the stables with him. Breathing the sweetness of summer hay calmed my heart a bit, but I still seethed.

"I saw all that," Charlie said as he pitched hay into a manger. Rain pelted the roof. Horses shifted in their stalls, and a brown cow looked over at me.

"'Twas only Robert. George even said, 'please,' to me. I warrant when those two meet the mudhole, they will rue the day they pleaded for the honor of meeting the train."

"Please, I'm a-needing Jacob's mule, Barney. Need to hustle home."

"In this tempest?" Charlie asked while Seamus brought out Barney. "I could harness a team and take you in a wagon."

"No, thank you. Only fetching more weaving."

"Up you go." Seamus laced his fingers together, cupping his hands for my foot.

The image of Robert bounced in my mind in time with Barney's gait. Just had to cut that foreigner down a notch. My hands tightened on the reins. That's exactly what I'd do.

I was shivering and bedraggled by the time I led Barney back into the settlement's stables, but my weaving and hatchet were snug in a piece of oilcloth.

"Merciful heavens!" Seamus grabbed Barney's reins. "Into the kitchen with ye. You'll catch your death. It's dry clothing and hot tea you're needing."

"I'll be fine."

"That's what me mum said, God rest her soul. A week later I carried her coffin."

I splattered through the mud to the kitchen. Blast it all! Why hadn't I packed a dry dress?

"Unless you borrow a corset, nothing of mine will fit you." Lizzie didn't even look up from the pie dough she was rolling out. "But you'll not step farther into this kitchen with those muddy boots."

"Come. We'll take the back passage." Janie took me up a narrow back staircase to the room she shared with Lizzie. "I've only one to spare. You'll be a-needing me to button up the back. Lizzie's got so many petticoats; she won't miss one. Nor a pair of clean drawers."

I shrugged off my clothes, and Janie helped me into her Turkey red calico flecked with tiny yellow flowers. I added dry drawers and a petticoat edged with gathered lace. Except for my braid and wider waist, I looked like a true sister to Lizzie.

"Best shake loose your hair if'n you want it to dry. You can sneak down the servants' way to your sewing."

"Thank you. I'm obliged."

I stitched all morning by the window, shaping pillows and hemming a lap robe. Sometime after the noon dinner, the wagons filled with wet gentlemen rolled up to the veranda. Boots slapped the stairs, and I jumped up to completely close the door. Wouldn't be seemly for some foreign gent to see me with my hair to my rear. Who should be standing outside the doorway but Charlie, holding two carpetbags and wearing a strange expression.

"Beg your pardon, Miss Viney." His eyes flitted over my hair. "I think I turned east instead of heading west." He backed away as I slammed the door.

Why were my cheeks flaming? Charlie made me feel like I was wearing only my chemise. I quicklike braided my hair and looked down at my hatchet, resting at the bottom of my sewing basket. I'd better make haste before those wagons lit off again for Sedgemoor. I tucked the hatchet into the waistband of Lizzie's petticoat and slipped down the servants' stairs, past ladies' voices chirping in a side parlor.

"Needing the privy," I said to Lizzie, and pulled her shawl from a hook. She nodded at me as she carried off a tray laden with teacups and a teapot.

I slid into the stables and glanced about. Appeared all were inside filling their bellies. I wiped the wooden axles on the oldest-looking wagon with a gunnysack and inspected the wood. A few hairline cracks etched the one axle, but the other bore a deeper split. I sunk my hatchet into that crack. The fracture grew deeper and longer. Again, I struck. Using mud from the sack, I smeared the gouge. I reckoned when the wagon wallowed in the mudhole, Royal Robert and King George would discover my surprise. In such a slow moving wagon, a split axle wouldn't bring the gents any harm. I could see the wood snap, the rear of the wagon plop into the mud, and those gentlemen's red faces. They would have a wet walk home.

A river of rain swept over me as I huddled under Lizzie's shawl and dashed toward the inn. I was tugging on the door to the mudroom when someone shoved it open. Arms encircled me. George slammed the door and sank onto a small bench, pulling me on his lap.

"A quick kiss, my pet," George whispered in my ear. His scent of citrus and spices fogged my brain. His mouth met mine. His hands inched up my ribs.

I screeched and kicked. Lizzie's shawl fell away. The kitchen door opened.

Lizzie squealed. Seamus and Charlie rushed about her.

"Take your hands off her!" Seamus shouted.

Charlie pulled George away. "You've the wrong girl!"

I trembled, hoping none of them saw the bulge of the hatchet beneath my skirt.

"How dare you!" Lizzie moved toward me, but I ran up the servants' stairs.

God bless Mrs. Johnstone, whose voice calling for order rose above Lizzie's. I slammed the door in my sewing room and dragged my sleeve across my lips. Hang that Englishman! His hands told me that he was making free with my sister. I hoped he would drown in that mudhole. Someone knocked on the door, and my stomach dropped to my knees.

"It's me. Janie." She flitted through the door. "Oh, Laws. If'n Lizzie hadn't those ladies to serve, she'd skin you."

"I have to shuck this red calico. I'll not be mistaken for Lizzie again."

"Your dress is almost dry. I'll bring it up later."

After Janie left, I hid the hatchet in my sewing basket and plopped on the chair, finishing my sewing. My insides felt all twisted . . . thankful for Charlie and Seamus delivering me, mad at George and Lizzie, and a little sad. If our mama had lived, she would talk sense into Lizzie. And explain to me Charlie's queer look. 'Twas evening before Janie returned with my dress.

"Be careful. Lizzie's still fit to hang you. Not even George's sweet talk calmed her."

"He and Robert drive off?"

"Nope. They whined and fussed about the rain until Mr. Hill sent Charlie and Seamus."

Mercy! My trick would fall on those two. I saw the flash of Charlie's hands as he pulled George off me.

"When did they leave?"

"Hmm, about an hour ago. Goin' take a right while to pull those wagons through the mud."

"Reckon so." A war divided me. Part of me shouted: Leave 'em! They're foreigners, too! But another part saw Seamus helping me onto Jake and Robert's wagon spraying Seamus with mud. Felt like someone was pinching and pulling me. By now they might be mired in the mudhole with a broken axle. But what help would I be? Thunder rattled the windowpanes. And how would I explain my arrival? *Just out for a little ride, boys.*

"Thank you, Janie. Be seeing you in the morning."

"Watch out for Lizzie!" she called after me.

I walked down the main stairway, head up and eyes straight forward. The gents in their frock coats and ladies wearing bustles stared at me from their horsehair seats in the parlor. I nodded at them, and brushed past more gents chattering on the veranda. Reckon I'd rather pass through a horde of foreigners than face my sister.

When I reached the stables, I lit off on Barney. Rain slapped my face. Wind tore apart my braid. I dug my heels into that mule. Mud splattered my skirt.

"Move, boy, move!" If I reached them soon enough, might spare them a broken axle. Mud pelted my legs. Lightning haloed the mountains and thunder churned the air.

Barney balked. He brayed and bucked.

"You stop that!"

If only I had on a pair of Jacob's britches and not a skirt riding halfway up my legs. My arms shook from clenching the reins. Lightning snagged a tree to the right of me, and Barney bolted. We clattered across the wooden planks bridging the Clear Fork and sighted lanterns. Up ahead, sandstone jutted out of the hillside as the road rounded a curve. Water oozing from the rock kept the road muddy, and the rain had created a pond. Above the storm I heard horses screaming.

I clung to saplings as I slid down the embankment, trying to skirt the mudhole and the heaving horses. Seamus leapt for a bridle, dodged hooves. Charlie tugged on the other horse sinking into the mud. Green briars ripped my sodden skirt. My feet slipped on wet leaves. I clung to an elderberry bush so as not to tumble against the rocks littering the hillside. My legs quivered.

By the time I stepped back onto the road, Charlie and Seamus had unhitched the team and tied the horses to trees. They stood under the narrow rock ledge, staring at me through a curtain of rain.

"Merciful heavens!" Seamus cried.

"Miss Viney?" Charlie stammered.

"Tarnation! Move over." I ran between them and out of the downpour. "I thought you might be a-needing my help."

"But how did you know to come?" Charlie asked.

Oh, how I hated his question. I'd been dreaming up lies all the way here, but looking into their trusting eyes pulled the plug. I set to bawling.

"I did it! I notched the axle. I hate that Robert. And George. Cussed curs."

"You did what?" Charlie asked.

"I whacked the axle with my hatchet! I'd like to ship those two, and all you foreigners, back to England. Thought Robert'd get in trouble for busting the wagon. Thought all those highfalutin guests'd be stuck in Sedgemoor. Wanted to spoil the grand opening." I gulped air between my sobs.

Charlie kept staring at me like I was bewitched.

"You've pluck," Seamus said. "Aye, a plucky lass."

"And now you'll tell the Hills, and they'll hate me. And Mrs. Hill's most like a mama to me." Finally, I sneezed and that shut me up. Charlie handed me his white handkerchief.

"It's clean. So why *did* you come if you would send us back to England?"

"'Cause I'm beholden to you. You all rescued me from King George." I blew my nose and wiped my face. "Had to repay your kindness somehow." Tree limbs chattered in the wind.

"But what can *you* do?" Charlie asked. Seamus still stared at me like I was one of his blessed saints. Thunder rumbled east of us.

"Haven't you fellars learned anything about mountain folk? We may look forward to bartering goods from your commissary, and come to your dances, but many folks feel like I do. Men hate to see the game fleeing. Riles them that you ask them to fence their hogs. Others like to be shut of those prissy guests. If'n you go knocking on some doors asking for help, they might not hear you knocking."

"So?" Charlie shrugged his shoulders.

"But if *I* go to them, they'll come. Janie's folks live up that holler. I'll walk in and ask for help."

"Nay." Seamus shook his head. "We'll ride Tom." He trotted toward a team and unbuckled their harness.

Felt queer standing there alone next to Charlie with my wet dress clinging to me. Temperature was falling, and the rain had slacked to a drizzle. I commenced shivering.

"How unkind of me." Charlie shook off his jacket and helped me into it. Felt odd to be treated such.

"Ready," Seamus called. He lifted me onto the horse and climbed in front. "Hold on. Which way?"

"A quarter mile to the right." I pressed my cheek against his wool jacket that smelled of horses and leather. I could feel the weave of the cloth, some sort of twilled pattern.

"Just a wee stream," Seamus whispered to the horse as we crossed the creek sweeping over the trail. A light glowed in the cabin's window, and the hounds set to baying. A door opened.

"Stop here. Let them hear my voice." I slid off the horse and ran up the porch steps.

"It's me. Viney Walker. Needing your help, Mr. Slone!" I rattled off my tale to Janie's pa. In no time, he and I were sitting on a wagon seat, following Seamus back to the road.

Fingers of mist rose from the gully, and thin clouds glazed the moon. The smell of damp earth and wet leaves surrounded us. When we reached the mudhole, Charlie stepped up and lifted me from the wagon seat. Suddenly, I went limp from all the commotion of the day. Trouble brought on by me. Charlie's arms steadied me, and I looked up into his face spattered with mud.

"Are you going to tell the Hills on me?" I asked, wondering if I appeared as scruffy as he did.

"Hmm, might." His hands fell away, but I could make out his smile.

I staggered a bit, and he gripped my shoulder. "Perhaps I should escort you back to the settlement?"

I shook my head. "Headed home."

"You did it for Seamus, didn't you?"

"Can't abide Robert."

"Neither can I." Charlie squeezed my hand. He hoisted me onto Barney's back.

On the ride back, I pinched myself to in order to stay awake. Finally, Barney stopped at our barn door, and I shut him in his stall. I collapsed on a pile of straw, still wearing Charlie's jacket and remembering the feeling of his hand on mine.

CHAPTER ELEVEN

One day a hotel is built, a summer settlement begins . . .
[in] *the mountains hitherto secluded from the outer*
world . . . a host of evils follows.

EMMA BELL MILES, *The Spirit of the Mountains*

Queer how I dreamed about snakes that night in the barn. Snakes spilling out of dignitaries' pockets. Snakes like ribbons roped about the ladies' bonnets. Set me to thinking as I lay there the next morning listening to Barney snuffle about his manger for the last bits of hay. The barn door opened.

"Viney!" Jacob halted and a smile slid across his face. "Well now, ain't that Charlie's jacket you're wearin'? Never thought I'd catch *you* in the hay mound."

I'd been so weary that I'd forgotten what I wore.

"I always reckoned Lizzie'd be the one who'd be *a-needing* to wed. So a fellar finally caught your eye. Reckon I best speak to him if'n things gone this far."

"Don't!" My face reddened. "You got it wrong! Charlie lent me his jacket. Just so tired, I never made it to the cabin. Fell asleep here."

"Do tell." Jacob smirked.

I had to take his thoughts off of me.

That queer look on Charlie's face when he saw my hair down flickered before me.

"Jacob, how do you know when a fellar's truly courting you?" I wondered if Jacob heard about George's attack. "How did Pa treat Mama?" Jacob sank down next to me and twisted a piece of straw around a finger.

"I recollect little things. The way Pa looked at Mama. He'd pick her the first violets. Or bring her honeycomb from a bee tree. Seen him wrap a shawl around her when she shivered."

He tugged on the sleeve of Charlie's jacket, and I looked away. Cindy Lou stuck her head over the stall boards and bellowed. Barney shifted in his stall.

"Reckon we've work to do." Jacob handed me the milk bucket.

While my hands stripped Cindy's udder of her milk, my mind sifted through Jacob's words and yesterday's troubles. I froze. My sewing basket with the hidden hatchet was still at the inn.

I sent Jacob on to the Grand Opening, saying I had a headache and would come later. 'Twas true. Between plotting on how to retrieve that basket and how to work my next idea, my brain pounded. I heeded Lizzie's warning not to humiliate her with my shabby clothes.

After scrubbing away yesterday's mud, I left my ripped dress to soak in a bucket. Last night's wind had swept the skies of clouds and crisped the air. A body couldn't feel downcast with purple asters and golden leaves bordering the view. I buttoned up my chestnut brown–checked dress and rummaged in a tiny splint basket with a lid that Aunt Idy had woven. Lizzie had left a handful of wooden hairpins that Jacob had carved for her. I coiled my dark blond braid into a crown like Janie wore and pinned it. I suddenly wished I had a few curls to soften my face. Foolishness, I scolded myself.

Taking a basket and a gunnysack, I marched to the edge of the corn patch and squatted down next to the rock pile. I began lifting rocks, peering about. A big black snake hid in these rocks, and plenty of mornings I'd watched him sun himself. Harmless rascal, but he could puff himself up right quick when threatened. City folks would think him dangerous.

"You're coming to the Grand Opening," I told the snake as I stuffed him into a poke and placed it in the basket on top of Charlie's jacket. With folks thinking Charlie was courting me, they'd never suspect I wanted to frighten away the English.

Gents with top hats and ladies with tiny waists milled about the Tabard Inn's lawn. The swirl of color put me in mind of leaves turning in the eddies of a river. The smell of fresh bread and roast mutton made my stomach grumble. After saying my howdys, I headed for the veranda.

A train of chairs stood near the railing. Yesterday I had noticed pots of ostrich ferns stationed at either end. While no one watched, I tucked that gunnysack beneath the drooping fronds and untied the opening. I figured that after the sun warmed the poke, the snake would wiggle out. A bell rang and I skipped over to where Jacob stood with Lucas's sister, Hazel. Charlie and Seamus stood nearby.

A man in a white robe with gold-embroidered crosses and holding a Bible walked onto the veranda. Must be their preacher. A passel of gray-haired gentlemen and a few ladies filed after him and settled on the chairs. Mr. Thomas Hughes sat in the middle. The preacher held up his arms. With the autumn leaves flaming over the hills and his flowing robes, 'twas like a scene from the Book of Revelation. He called out "Old Hundredth," and the gents lit into the hymn:

"From all that swell below the skies,
Let the Creator's praise arise,
Let the Redeemer's name be sung,
Through every land, by every tongue."

Real solemn and earnest those gents were, and afterward the preacher read two psalms and prayed a blessing over the town. That was it for the preaching! No talk of a coming judgment or hell.

I nudged Jacob. "Couldn't they find a better preacher? What religion is this?"

"Episcopalian," he sounded out the word. "This here man's a bishop. A mighty important preacher from Knoxville."

I shook my head. Even their preacher couldn't work up a spit. One by one, the gentlemen stood up and yammered on about this fine settlement. How they'd built a New Jerusalem and that today was the beginning of a grand experiment. This town, now named Rugby, was to be a Christian Social Community. The railing hid the base of the potted fern, but I watched as the sun inched along the veranda.

Finally, Mr. Hughes stood above us. Next to the pasty-faced politicians, Mr. Hughes glowed. All week I had observed him flit about like a scarlet tanager, directing folks. I could tell he wasn't a selfish man, and I could understand why folks sidled up to him. He had a mortal sweet way with words, and could whip up their enthusiasm like a fiddler set feet to dancing. I just wanted him to take his town back to England.

"We must stand shoulder to shoulder and work with our minds and hearts for the same great end," he preached.

Whose end? I wanted to ask. He spoke of folks coming from Boston and Chattanooga, Ireland and England, but what about the people already living here?

Mr. Hughes tossed out phrases filled with grandeur. "We have made up our minds to put our hands earnestly to work. We want to establish a community based on respect and equality."

Is that so? Tell that to King George and Royal Robert, who won't dirty their hands. And what was happening here before you all arrived? We didn't need foreigners telling us how to live. Most times neighbors pitched in and lent a hand when a body needed help.

"As a community, we must have something in common. In the first place, there is this lovely corner of God's earth entrusted to us."

I could feel my blood temperature rising. Mr. Hughes talked on about not spoiling these hills, but never made mention of the trees sawed for his town. Or of the wildflowers and herbs trampled by his settlers. I glanced about. A passel of mountain men stood in the back, lips pressed together, arms crossed. They were listening to Mr. Hughes's words about common property, a cooperative commissary, and hard work, but they weren't reaching for the baited hook.

"Fine talking," Samuel Jackson muttered. "But all they's done is complain about my hogs running through their garden pretties. We've always runned hogs in these woods."

"Built themselves a *tennis court* where I used to hunt turkeys," Miles Harlan said. "Toms strutted their mating dance in that spot since my granddaddies' time. No sense at all."

Mr. Hughes raised his arms and concluded, "Our hope is to plant on these highlands a community of gentlemen and ladies in which the humblest members will live by the labor of their own hands."

I snorted. Several mountain men shifted their feet and glanced sideways at each other. Except for Charlie and Seamus, there were too many settlers like King George and Royal Robert, who were more interested in tennis and tea drinking. These rich folk had heaps to learn about work before they could live by their hands.

A woman screamed. "SNAKE!"

"A COBRA!" Another lady screeched and fainted. Her feathered hat flew off the veranda.

I jumped onto a bench but could only see swooshing skirts and flapping frock coats. By thunder, those gents could step quickly.

"Just a black snake," one of the gents hollered, but nobody paid him any mind.

"Fetch a hoe!" Mr. Hughes ordered. A man dashed toward a shed.

"Too late!" Mr. Hill shouted. "Went down a knothole."

"Find him!" a lady cried, and collapsed.

I eased through the crowd, aiming for the kitchen. I had to rescue my sewing basket while folks wrestled with that dangerous snake.

Lizzie was heaping roast mutton and ham onto platters while Janie filled bowls with green beans. Lizzie grinned.

"Come for your basket, didn't ye? She threw down a three-prong fork. "Mighty heavy thread you're usin'. Or maybe it's that new cuttin' tool."

I felt my blood sink to my toes. I *knew* Lizzie would snoop. Her skirts skimmed the floor, and she held out my basket.

"Now why would my little sister be a-needing a hatchet to sew pillows? Reckon you brought that snake, too."

My mouth went as dry as a cottonmouth's. Suddenly, Mrs. Johnstone bustled into the kitchen and pointed at me.

"Is she here to help?"

"No, ma'am—" I started.

"Then out with you! Girls, take in those platters. Carry in the bowls. Need to distract folks from that snake. Whoever played this prank will be caught."

"Yes, ma'am." Lizzie and Janie snatched up the dishes.

I fled to the stables, hoping to leave Charlie's jacket and then head for home. A forkful of hay about knocked me over as it tumbled through a hole in the loft floor. I jumped back, spitting hay and wiping my eyes.

"Y'all trying to kill me?"

"Joseph and Mary!" Seamus cried. He and Charlie clattered down the loft stairs.

"Why aren't you fellars out celebrating? I saw you listening to the speeches."

"Begging your pardon, miss, but shouldn't we be asking the same of you?" Seamus said. "We've extra animals to tend."

"Reckon so," I handed Charlie his jacket. "Thank you." Hay prickled my neck. "I best be going."

Seamus escorted me outside.

"Thank you for your help last night. You're a brave lassie." He plucked hay from my hair. "I know you hate that we've butchered your woods, but Mr. Hughes hopes that one day your people will be blessed by this settlement." Seamus closed the door, and I lit out toward the path to the woods.

Just then, Mrs. Hill and a squatty gentlemen rounded the corner of the Tabard, and I bit my lip.

"Reckon so. Best be off."

"Viney!" Mrs. Hill called. "I must speak with you."

My knees about buckled. I plodded toward them. The gent put me in mind of a pumpkin with spectacles perched on his fleshy, round face. I couldn't look at Mrs. Hill, but focused on the garnet brooch pinned to her collar. I wondered if they'd ship me to a jail in Knoxville or fine me the price of the axle. Either way, I would never hear Mrs. Hill's praises again.

"Mr. Foster, may I introduce Miss Viney Walker. She's the talented young lady who wove the coverlet for our rustic room. Viney, dear, I'd like you to meet Mr. Foster of Cincinnati."

"Please to meet you," I said, and gave him my hand. What did this gentleman want with me?

"A pleasure to meet you, Miss Walker," Mr. Foster said. His spectacles made his eyes appear larger, like I was staring into a cow's face. "I so admired the samples of your weavings in the inn. Amos and Margaret told me that no other person in these hills can surpass your artistry."

"Thank you, sir." I kept smiling, though my feet wanted to bolt. I couldn't tell by Mrs. Hill's expression whether she suspected I had played today's trick or harmed the wagon.

"Would you be willing to weave coverlets for my home in Cincinnati?" Mr. Foster asked. "And I want to tell my friends about you."

If you knew I hid that snake, you would surely tell your friends even more about me! I kept my eyes on my boot toes.

"Do say yes, dear. Mr. Foster would pay you well. And you must promise to weave more coverlets for the Tabard. We would like to furnish other rooms with local crafts; they would display the traditions of these hills," Mrs. Hill added.

"Yes, ma'am," I replied. My mind tumbled over such a proposal. Never in my born days had I dreamed of such. Just then a bevy of ladies swept over and started chattering. I turned to go, but Mrs. Hill caught my arm.

"Not staying for the revelry?" Mrs. Hill turned with me toward the path home.

"No, ma'am." Now I'd hear her rebuke. Most likely she was putting on a show for that Mr. Foster. My palms itched from sweating.

"I hope you accept the weaving job. You have a rare talent; share it with the flatlanders. Take pride in your mountain heritage."

"I'll be thinking on it, ma'am." Our feet swooshed

through the blanket of autumn leaves. I kept a-waiting for those dreaded words.

"The cash money would be handy. I know Lizzie sends little home." Mrs. Hill reached out and hugged me as we parted.

Mrs. Hill *didn't* know! But as riled as Lizzie was about George kissing me, would she remain silent?

CHAPTER TWELVE

My people everywhere on the borders of the mountain country are being laid hold of and swept away by the on coming tide of civilization that drown as many as it uplifts . . .

EMMA BELL MILES, *The Spirit of the Mountains*

I kept to the cabin as the days shortened and the fall rains fell. My feet pressed the treadles of my loom while my hands tossed the shuttle. I wanted to finish the coverlets by Christmas, before snow sealed the paths. By then, I hoped folks would stop gossiping about who hid the snake.

As angry as Lizzie had been about George kissing me, why hadn't she told? Or maybe she had, and that was why the Hills hadn't visited me. Those thoughts plagued me like this one thin thread in my warp that kept fraying and breaking. I didn't have the time to unwind the whole warp and replace it, seeing as I had promised that pumpkin-head fellar I would finish his coverlets by year's end. Every time I knotted that thread, I pondered my guilt and would resolve that come Sunday, I'd tell Mrs. Hill everything. Then the clouds would split open, turning the trail into mud, and my courage would melt. After all, I still wanted to find a way to send the foreigners packing before they built more houses.

One Sunday the clouds slipped eastward, leaving a dusting of snow. I paused in the barnyard with my steaming bucket of milk and gazed at the tree limbs etched against the lavender sky. The layers of clouds looked like they were holding down the sun, but then she poked up one finger, and then another and flung back the covers. Those sunrays glowed against the bottom of the cloud layers, turning them golden, like the sparkly flakes I had seen in rocks.

Today, I scolded myself. Today you tell Mrs. Hill. It was the Sabbath, and I didn't need any preacher to tell me that sin was gnawing at my heart.

I lit out after our dinner, but it was hard going. The mud had frozen into deep ruts, and my boots kept slipping on the slick bits of snow. I meandered along wishing I'd stayed by the hearth, when I heard hoofbeats drumming on the rock-hard dirt. I snuck behind a clump of pines, as I was in no mind to talk.

From around the bend I recognized Lizzie, looking just like an English lady. She wore a maroon velvet riding habit, and lace frothed at her cuffs and throat. A narrow bonnet with an ostrich feather topped her curls. George's horse trotted up next to Lizzie, and George leaned over and kissed her. Their laughter quivered in the air like the notes of the thrush's call. Ahead of me they paused where a small spring bubbled from the base of the hill. George tied their horses to a tree and lifted Lizzie down. She kept her hands on his shoulders.

"Today," she said. "You'll ask Jacob today."

"Yes." George pressed his lips to hers for a powerful long time. How did those two keep breathing? For the flick of a bee's wing, I wondered what such kissing would feel like.

"Now," Lizzie said. She skipped over to the spring, and George squatted down beside her. He dipped his cupped hands into the pool and pressed them to her lips. Three drops fell and streaked the bodice of her habit. Lizzie sipped, and then George's hands swallowed her chin. His thumbs stroked her cheeks. She dropped her riding crop and slid her arms around him.

"After our ride." He kissed her again.

I watched Lizzie's body relax. Like the spring at her feet, some current flooded through her. Her face softened as George's lips crept down her throat. I knew what had changed her countenance. Lizzie was in love. A boy had finally bound her heart and was squeezing her for all she'd give. I feared for my sister.

I recollected George's shaving scent fogging my mind, and his cheek brushing mine when he stole that kiss. My sister was a fool to yield to the likes of him! I dashed from the pines and skidded onto the road. The horses whinnied. George and Lizzie split apart.

"Right pretty day, isn't it?" I asked, and smiled. "Where y'all bound?"

Lizzie's eyes glowed like hot chestnuts. She picked up her riding crop, and I wondered if she'd lash it at me. George brushed leaves from his knees.

"Out for a bit of a ride." He studied me. "And yourself?"

"Off to see the Hills."

"Would you like a ride?" George asked. Lizzie glared at him.

I knew my sister wouldn't want me sitting with her, and I wasn't sharing any horse with King George.

"No, thank you. 'Tisn't far." I waved and walked away.

My toes were numb by the time I marched up the Hills' steps, but my brain blazed. Any fool could see that Lizzie was end-over-backward in love and was ready to be led into the hay mound. I had to do something to send George away before Jacob ordered a shotgun wedding.

"Viney! Come in, lamb." Mrs. Hill opened the door.

"Good afternoon. How y'all been?"

Seamus and Charlie looked up from the table where they shared tea with Mr. Hill. Shadows smudged Charlie's eyes, and worry pinched his face.

"Tarnation! Did someone die?" I asked.

"Not quite." Seamus jumped up and pulled out a chair for me. Such manners still felt queer.

"My father wrote," Charlie answered.

"And?"

"You've heard our advice, Charles. Why don't you read the letter to Viney." Mr. Hill pushed in his chair. "Could I interest you in a short walk, Maggie?" He helped Mrs. Hill into her coat and quietly shut the door.

In his strong English accent Charlie read:

"Dear Charles,

Your mother, brothers, and I are well, and we trust that you are, too. The London papers reported Rugby's fashionable opening ceremonies. They have also commented on the internal problems with the Board of Land Aid, and that until the gentlemen solve their differences, few farms will be available for purchase. I have little faith in your Mr. Hughes to solve this situation. I expect you to keep your word and look forward to seeing you this spring."

Charlie threw down the letter and leaned back in his chair.

"What that means is that I persuaded my father to pay for a year's apprenticeship, during which time I was to secure land and begin farming. Because the investors continue to argue about how to divide the land and what prices to charge, Seamus and I wait. If I am unable to satisfy my father's demands by April, then I must return home and pursue a career he chooses for me."

"Well, just tell him you won't leave!" I felt like a needle had pricked my finger, but I wasn't sure why. "He can't come fetch you home."

"And be disowned? Although my older brother will one day receive my family's estate, until then my father will probably provide me with a monthly allowance."

"Can't your brother share? Jacob'd never run me off. He's already hinting at building me a little cabin if'n Hazel says yes."

"Such are not the ways in England. The eldest son inherits *everything*. And I have five younger brothers. Even if my father divided the estate, there would never be enough land for each of us to earn a suitable income. This is why I came to Rugby, to purchase my own land. To be part of a community where everyone was equal. But if I can't buy a farm this spring, I must go home."

"Do Yankees abide by those ways?" I looked at Seamus. "Is that why you came here?"

"I suppose some families might hold to those traditions, but my da is a gardener and manages the stables for a wealthy family. I was hoping that here I'd be known for how hard I worked, and not scorned as Irish. In time I hoped to earn enough to buy a farm."

"What about King George and Royal Robert? Are they in the same fix?"

"Is that what you call them?" Seamus laughed.

"They'll be leaving eventually. They planned to only spend the year. Their fathers sent them over in order to develop manly character. When they return, their parents' bank accounts ensure good positions with some London firm," Charlie said.

Appeared the Lord would relieve me of those two, but the image of George kissing Lizzie's throat made me bite my lip.

"Does Lizzie know that George'll be leaving?" I asked. Seamus and Charlie exchanged glances.

"I don't know." Charlie folded his father's letter into tinier and tinier squares. "For the present all I can think about is how to alter my father's decision. He wants me to be a minister or doctor, anything but a farmer."

I hated seeing Charlie fret. "Why don't you buy a farm from someone on the ridge? That'd make your pa happy, right? I could ask about."

"Seamus and I have only saved enough for a few acres, and because we came as apprentices, the Land Board's farms should cost less." Charlie stuffed the letter in his waistcoat pocket. "At least, that's what they promised us."

Bits of blue flecked the gray wool tweed of the waistcoat. I told myself that next time I brewed indigo, I would dye some fleece and card it into some black wool. Make a tweed like that. It would look nice on Jacob.

"Reckon I'll just have to wait till spring," Charlie said, trying to imitate a Tennessee accent.

"Reckon so," Seamus added, and stood up. "Suppose I should be practicing those silly English tunes that Miss Ringgold asked me to learn for the party."

Charlie ran a finger along the edge of the table. "How do mountain folk celebrate the Christmas holidays?"

"We make merry on Old Christmas, January sixth. Have a jollification. Most years folks gather at our cabin. Jacob fiddles. We dance. A few fellars shoot off guns."

"Jacob already asked me to bring my fiddle to your gathering," Seamus said.

"You didn't tell me!" Charlie glowered.

Seamus shrugged his shoulders and shoved in his chair.

"So? Will you come, too?" I asked Charlie. "Might cheer you. Plenty of fiddling and food."

"Yes, I will, if you will please accompany me to Rugby's New Year's Eve party."

"I can't mingle with those lords and ladies! Just the sight of me will raise their noses." And I didn't want to risk irritating Lizzie.

"Just think of them as homesick lads needing dance partners. Please come." Charlie took my hand.

I snatched back my hand, my cheeks burning. "I reckon I can come." I turned to go.

"I should ride you home." Charlie stood up. "Mr. Hill said that folks spotted a panther not far from here. He's had us bring in the sheep every night and bolt the door."

"No. No, thank ye. I'll step lively." His offer reminded me of Lizzie and George. Folding my shawl about me, I slipped out the door and waved good-bye to the Hills as they walked from the barn.

Why, oh why had I said yes to Charlie's proposal? What would Lizzie say when she saw me trotting into that party? Blast it all! I had come to confess to Mrs. Hill and had plum forgotten to speak up. Seemed like every time I was around those lads, my own thoughts drained away. I halted, listening to the woods. My mind untangled the sounds of tree branches clicking against each other and rattling oak leaves. Two owls called to each other, and my heartbeat slowed. The panther hadn't come near our woods, yet.

Chapter Thirteen

We held hands like the Scots and sang "Auld Lang Syne" . . . celebrating health to the President and the Queen [Victoria].

THE RUGBEIAN

"**Y**ou ratty little . . . " I let go of my beater and pulled on a broken thread.

"What's wrong with you?" Jacob set down his fiddle. "Feel like I've been living with a bobcat. All you need is pointy ears."

"Then maybe I'd better start growling!" I tied a weaver's knot and stomped up the ladder to the loft.

The black-eyed peas I'd eaten for good luck in the New Year sat like gravel in my stomach. In an hour Charlie would arrive to walk me to his highfalutin' party. None of my dresses were good enough for his society, my hair fell like limp flax, and my hands were chapped from washing clothes. This was one of those times when I longed for a mama to straighten my collar, brush my hair, and whisper advice in my ear. Jacob didn't understand.

"I don't know what to wear," I shouted down to Jacob.

Snow struck the loft window, and a gust of wind shook the shingles.

"You should've asked Lizzie. Or Mrs. Hill."

I pulled my blue-checked dress from its hook. If only I had asked Jacob to bring home a bit of trim from the commissary, but we had used most of our credit to barter for flour, salt, and sugar, plus a new harness. I fussed with my hair. If I wound it into a bun, I would look like Aunt Alta. Lizzie would scoff at a braid, and a crown was what serving girls often wore. I managed to roll my hair into a sausage like Lizzie wore and pinned it at the back of my neck. Was being proper worth all this bother?

While lacing my pinch-the-toes boots, I heard bells. Jacob heaved open the door. I flung my coat and shawl around me and raced out after him. Steam puffed from the horses' nostrils as Seamus pulled the reins and stopped a cherry red sleigh by our porch. One of the lads had strung tiny brass bells about the horses' necks. Charlie hopped out and gave me his hand.

"Mr. Hughes ordered this cutter for the inn. Thought it would be handy for driving into Sedgemore. Mr. Hill allowed us to use it tonight. We can outrun any panther that might stalk us."

"Grand enough for Queen Mauve, the fairy queen," Seamus said. "Slip under these blankets now. 'Tis so cold, it feels like we're in Boston."

Charlie tucked the blankets around us, and I hunkered down, so that only my face showed. We were three chickens snug on our roost. Seamus slapped the reins, and we skimmed away.

The cutter bucked a bit over a few rough bumps and ruts, but the snow had been packed into a slick trail. The runners swooshed, and the snow squeaked. I felt like the Lord had sewn wings on my shoulders. I was a hawk gliding through snow-covered hemlocks while above me stars glittered like chips of ice.

"Here." Charlie slipped a small package beneath the covers and pressed it into my mittens. "Happy New Year."

Though his head still faced forward, I could tell Seamus was watching. I peeked under the blankets, and a length of ribbon slid out of the tissue paper.

"Green. To match your eyes," Charlie said.

All I could see was Charlie tying a ribbon beneath Lizzie's curls. What did this mean? Was I merely a substitute for the girl he longed for? My stomach twisted.

"Thank you." My tongue felt starched.

"'Twill look lovely in your hair, Miss Viney." Seamus's eyes lingered on mine. "Take heart, you'll be the flower of the flock."

I felt more like a lamb among wolves when Charlie escorted me into the Tabard. Someone had hung pine swags with ribbons on the tall wooden entry doors. More pine boughs decorated the stairway and the mantel of the fireplace in the parlor. Janie Slone met us in the hallway. She glanced at Charlie's hand on my arm.

"Viney! Lizzie didn't tell me you were coming. Here, let me take y'all's coats."

"She doesn't know. Can I speak with you for a moment?"

"Surely."

"I'll wait," Charlie said as I followed Janie around the corner.

"Tie this on me, please." The cold had stiffened my fingers. "Is Lizzie serving?"

Janie fussed with the ribbon and brought it under my sausage roll.

"I hope that holds." She poked my hair into place. "Lizzie serve? Your sister's aiming to frolic. She cozied up to that Miss Ringgold wearing the red jewels. She gave Lizzie a real gown. Even lent a couple of Lizzie's friends some of her old dresses. Which gent gave you the ribbon?"

"Charlie." Felt queer to be naming him, like that length of ribbon tied a piece of me to him.

"Hmmm. Saw them lads choosing this ribbon. Seems they's hitched together like horses. Listen up. When you're moving through that parlor, mind that round green ball hanging from the ceiling. 'Tis mistletoe. English gents can take a kiss from any gal caught beneath it."

"I reckon Lizzie and George lingered there." We rounded the corner where Charlie stood.

"Lizzie and George don't need no mistletoe." Janie rolled her eyes.

Charlie offered me his arm, and we marched into the pine-scented room. Dozens of candles burned on every window ledge and table. The candles' glow dappled the room like sunlight through forest leaves. Clusters of foreigners chatted near a platter of small cakes. The gentlemen's satin waistcoats shimmered as they moved in and out of the shadows. All the English girls wore bell-shaped crinolines under their taffeta skirts. I felt like a wilted daylily among a bouquet of roses.

Lizzie shone in blood red satin with a neckline dipping so low, I thought she would take a chill. Little lacy frills puffed over her shoulders, and her bustle cascaded like a waterfall off her behind. She fluttered a green silk fan, and George's locket sailed on her bosom. Our gazes met, and her locket bobbed as her breathing quickened. Her eyes were black ice waiting to cut my steps. Had we come to the point where the threads of sisterhood had snapped? The other girls twittered.

"Would you like some refreshment?" Charlie asked, and guided me toward a cloth-covered table. I fingered the linen edged with lace.

"From Ireland." Charlie filled little glass cups with a fruity-smelling drink. Bits of oranges floated in my cup.

"I thought the English didn't fancy the Irish." Only once, when visiting the Hills, had I eaten an orange. I rolled the beaded segment across my teeth, sucking down the sweetness.

"They don't, but Englishwomen know good linen. This was probably woven by a countrywoman like yourself, while her daughters crocheted the lace."

I ran my hands across the smoothly woven linen, hearing the woman's feet pushing her loom pedal. Most likely she had grown the flax and broken it out in her barnyard. I wished I could meet her and talk.

For the first time, I noticed that unlike the other gents with tucked bibs on their shirts and gold cuff links, Charlie wore a plain shirt with his waistcoat. His cuticles were cracked, and calluses darkened his palms. His hands matched Jacob's. He saw me staring and stuffed his hands into his pockets.

"I'm sorry that my hands are so rough. I've been sharing my gloves with Seamus. He needs to protect those musical fingers."

"Might have an extra pair at home. I knitted Jacob some new ones this fall."

"Thank you. I would highly value the work of your hands."

I felt red coloring my cheeks.

Two other lads strolled up, and Charlie introduced me to Nicholas and Christian. Glancing about, I saw two of Lizzie's friends. Despite the additional English lasses, must have been three gents to every girl. Seamus tuned his fiddle while another lad sat at a large piano.

"Will you give me this dance, Miss Viney?" Nicholas asked, and offered me his hand.

"Please save one for me," Christian said.

"Why, yes." I glanced at Charlie. His eyes glinted in the candlelight.

"Please reserve one for me as well," he said, and sipped his punch.

Nicholas and I joined up with another couple in the queerest dance. It was called "Rufty Tufty" and was danced to one particular tune. Nicholas whispered the steps as we minced about, staring into each other's eyes. I felt like I was circling a rooster, holding his gaze until I could nab him for the pot. We never did swing or move on to dance with another couple. Seamus looked bored playing the same tune repeatedly. With Christian, I danced "Hit and Miss," a dance as silly as its name. Didn't these folk know how to frolic?

"Thank you, Miss Viney." Christian bowed. "A pleasure to meet such a smooth dancer."

"Thank you." I didn't trust my tongue to spit out proper speech, and I didn't think this fellow would like me comparing him to a rooster. As Charlie lead me to the dance floor I overheard two of the English girls.

"Doesn't she know that green ribbon looks dreadful with her blue dress? She looks like a frog sitting in a puddle. Hard to imagine that *she* is Lizzie's sister."

"Dressed like a servant, at *our* party," a girl in a sky blue gown said. "At least the others tried to look decent."

I clenched my hands so hard that my nails bit into my palms. Charlie's neck reddened, and I knew he'd heard them, too. Appeared the English gals were as arrogant as their lads.

"Ladies and gentlemen." The sky blue lady clapped her hands. A necklace of glittering rubies skimmed across her chest. Seeing as she was about the same size as Lizzie, and her dress was similar, I reckoned she was Miss Ringgold. The layers of satin rustled as she glided to the center of the room. Hadn't anyone warned her about that mistletoe? She nodded at Lizzie and George and held out her gloved hands.

"I have the honor of making a special announcement." She took one of Lizzie's hands and rested it on George's pink palm, pulling the couple beneath the mistletoe.

All the lads stared at Lizzie, aflame in her gown. I could feel their heat rising around me as they feasted on her slim white arms and that low neckline. I felt like a cornshuck doll compared to my sister, but at least corn was good for something.

"Tonight I announce the engagement of Miss Elizabeth Walker to George Sterling Elsworth."

I gasped. This had to be a trick. George might promise my sister a wedding, but he would never make good on it.

George slipped a ring sparkling with a green gem onto Lizzie's finger. She circled her arms around his neck, and they kissed until I thought they'd faint. The ladies laughed. The lads cheered.

I glanced at Charlie, leaning against the table with his arms crossed over his chest. Had he known about this when he invited me? Were his fingers still missing the feel of Lizzie's hair?

"Choose a partner for 'Picking Up Sticks'!" the caller said. "Longways sets for six."

Charlie offered me his arm and marched me to where Lizzie and George had found Robert and Miss Ringgold.

"May we join you?" Charlie asked, and steered me into place.

I stared at him, but his eyes were deep water, one of those bends in the river's current that can suck you down. The others scowled at us for tainting their set. My hands trembled until I glanced at Miss Ringgold's pudgy fingers, and Robert's and George's hands.

Not a nick or blister, soft and white, without calluses or cracks. They had never washed dishes or milked a cow in the frigid morning air. Even Lizzie's hands had more color than these foreigners', which were as lifeless as a corpse's. When I lifted my eyes to Charlie's, I felt his current of defiance swirl me away. Who were these people that I should tremble?

Seamus started a scratchy tune, and we lit into a most confusing dance. Swapping places along our lines, over and over. I gazed into those men's faces like I was a red-tailed hawk circling the ridge. George and Charlie pulled me every which way while Lizzie's frown deepened. Suddenly Miss Ringgold grabbed my hand, and we commenced skipping in and out between the men, weaving a figure eight. We flew, with Lizzie in the lead and me at the end. Put me in mind of playing crack-the-whip during our school days.

I felt my hair tumbling. I snatched at the descending roll flowing over my back. Pins clattered onto the polished boards. Like a bay mare's tail, my hair rode out behind me. The girls gasped. Robert smirked. Charlie bent over and picked up the pins.

Blood rushed to my cheeks. If these had been my people, someone would jest and folks would simply smile and start another dance. But these foreigners stared at me, and I wanted to melt through a knothole.

"Here." Charlie put one hand on my waist and another on my shoulder. "Do the same." Seamus fiddled a different tune, which sounded like swooping swallows.

Charlie whirled me about the room, dancing closer to the open doorway. We slid under the archway and into the hall. Panting, he handed me my hairpins.

I dashed up to Janie's room and braided my hair, tying it with Charlie's ribbon. Had Seamus thought of playing that sweeping dance on his own? I found my coat and shawl and joined Charlie on the veranda steps. Head arched back, he gazed at the endless sweep of stars.

"At home I could climb a small rise and see from one

end of the horizon to the other. I wish I could see the whole sky again."

"Homesick?" I curled my toes in my boots against the cold.

"Yes. Your mountains are lovely, but I miss the sea. The smell of salt air. The sound of waves thundering on rocks. I love watching banks of storm clouds rise across the water and spread over our fields. And it's never this cold."

"Queer. Without these hills I'd feel like a rabbit with no cover and an owl swooping over me."

"I'm sorry I chose green." Charlie leaned against a white pillar. "Seamus and I thought it was your favorite color. I suppose we should have remembered about matching ribbons with frocks."

"Don't pay those girls any mind," I had to fill up the silence. "No clouds tonight. What does that forecasting tool you have say?"

"Would you like to see my barometer? We could go check it."

I could tell by his voice that I'd led him away from the homesickness and the mishap.

"Surely." I shivered. "Can't stand in this cold much longer."

"I'm so sorry. I should have thought of that." He reached for my hand.

"Race you!" I dashed toward the stables. It felt good to run, snow squeaking beneath my boots, lungs burning from sucking in the frigid air. Charlie sprinted in front of me and hurried to light two lanterns. The straw-slicked floor glowed golden, and I held my hands near the lantern's warmth.

Charlie removed a round wooden disk with a glass globe from a post. A brass ring that held in the glass sparkled in the lantern light.

"See the silver plate with the markings: SQUALLS, RAIN, CHANGE, and FAIR? Every morning I set that gold needle, matching it to the black one. The black needle moves up or down according to the air pressure. I write down my observations in my weather journal. This morning it had risen, but now it is falling toward CHANGE."

Just like my life, I thought. I stared at the little needles connected to a spring inside the globe. How did air make that spring move?

"Probably it will snow or rain tomorrow," Charlie added.

"What do those numbers mean? And all those little black marks . . . TWENTY-NINE . . . THIRTY and such."

"Scientists use those numbers to measure the air pressure."

"You mean air's pressing against us like a coverlet?"

"Yes. That is why sometimes the summer heat feels so oppressive."

"How'd you come by all this learning?"

"Books. My uncle Charles gave me the aneroid barometer and a copy of Luke Howard's paper on the classification of clouds. He said they would be handy for a farmer. Though I'm beginning to wonder if I'll ever own a farm." Charlie flopped down on a pile of straw.

"Surely the Land Board will sort itself out by spring." I slid my back along the boards of a stall and leaned against it. "And if you and Seamus join your savings, you'll manage to buy something. Might not be a place as grand as your pa's."

Charlie laughed. "George is the one from a manor house. His father even owns land in Ireland. My father's farm is small and lovely. Stone walls that ride the hills to the sea. Primroses and foxgloves nestled along the banks of the burn, or creek as you call it."

Charlie rattled on about wide, gnarled oaks, skylarks soaring upward until they were only a speck against the blue, and the Harvest Home celebration when he rode high up on the wagons of grain. Finally he stopped and twirled a piece of straw with his finger.

"If you miss it so, why don't you want to go back?" I asked.

"None of it will be mine. *None* of it." He raked his hair behind his ears.

I opened my mouth just as Seamus walked into the stable. For a heartbeat I thought he looked envious, but then he laughed.

"Such an odd way to court a lass. Showing her your weather tool! The grand folk are dining and talking about sleigh rides. We'd best whisk Miss Viney home." He removed the harness from its hook. Charlie hurried to bring in the team.

For some odd reason, when Charlie dropped the bolt into the tongue of the sleigh, I saw George slipping that ring onto Lizzie's finger. "Do y'all think George truly means to marry my sister? Take her off the ridge?"

"George and I attended Rugby School together," Charlie

said. "He came here as something of a blackguard, but Lizzie *has* changed him. I believe his intentions are honest." Charlie gave me his hands and helped me into the cutter.

"But George chums about with that Robert," I said. Charlie climbed in near me, and Seamus settled into the driver's side.

"Robert encourages George to take pleasure in whatever pleases him. After all, their parents are across the ocean. Why not make merry?"

I sank down in the blanket. That's what worried me. George might say anything to convince Lizzie to join him in the hay mound.

"But will George marry Lizzie before he leaves? And take her home with him?" If they didn't wed before he left, I worried that Lizzie would find herself nursing a babe on our front porch.

"If George wants to wed Lizzie, he'd have to do it here. His parents would not agree to him marrying a servant. 'Tis beneath his status."

I would have slapped George if I had heard such talk from his mouth. Lizzie might be foolish, but she was as good as any of those arrogant boys. Why couldn't she understand how these foreigners looked down on us?

"But if they marry, then George'll make Lizzie live in England." My breath froze as frost and gathered on the edges of my shawl. "I'll never see her again." In the past Lizzie had dreamed of moving to Knoxville, a far piece for a body to travel, but I had reckoned she would visit.

"Aye." Seamus spoke. "Many's the Irish lad or lass who

crossed the Atlantic knowing they'd never again see the faces of their kin."

No, my heart beat. No. These foreigners had sawed my trees, trampled my wildflowers, and lured my sister into town. But I wouldn't let King George sail Lizzie from our hills. Think, I told myself, think of some way to stop him.

CHAPTER FOURTEEN

The fiddler and the banjo player are well treated
and beloved among them, like the minstrels
of feudal days.

EMMA BELL MILES, *The Spirit of the Mountains*

O ld Christmas brought Lizzie home. She traipsed in wearing a bodice stitched from twilled wool the color of plums, and many more yards fell in a pleated bustle while a deep ruffle swirled about her ankles.

"I wanted to twist your neck for showing up at *my* party. Looking like a cornshuck doll." Lizzie slammed the door. "Don't even know how to pin up your hair. If'n you want to frolic with your betters, I need to teach you how to dress."

"And good afternoon to you, too." I spooned corn bread batter into a tin pan and set it in a Dutch oven. "If'n Charlie hadn't invited me, I'd not have come."

"Charlie." Lizzie snorted. "Not much better than that Paddy. What *do* you see in him?"

"They are my friends. And you accepted Charlie's ribbons quick enough."

"Folks don't think that Charlie's just your friend." Lizzie

glanced at me before fussing with her hair. "But he was handy, made George propose sooner than I had hoped."

"And now George *claims* he'll marry you." I pushed aside the memory of them kissing at the spring and the way Lizzie's face melted with yearning. Instead I ran my fingers across the wool of her dress, counting the threads and calculating whether the weaver used a four- or six-harness loom. Had she used that seashell dye I'd heard of to give that wool such a deep purple?

"Jacob gave us his blessing. We are planning a summer wedding at the inn. George says he'll book a suite on the steamer to England for our wedding trip. No mountain shivaree for me. Only fine linen and china, and listening to concerts on the ship. I'm even to have a trousseau." Lizzie pranced about the cabin. Her ring flashed in the sunlight.

"You don't even know what a trousseau is!" I scrambled inside my brain to recollect what the word meant.

"Do so. Amelia told me about hers. Petticoats, camisoles, and drawers sewn from fine lawn, with real Belgian and French lace. New frocks. Kid gloves. Embroidered bed linens, too."

"Amelia?" I hoped Lizzie would allow me to feel that lawn; I'd never spun cotton.

"Miss Ringgold to you."

"If you're turning your back on mountain ways, what brought you here to celebrate Old Christmas?"

"'Cause I *want* to! It's still my home, too!"

Lizzie minded the door, greeting kith and kin. Soon children chased each other, women jiggled babies, and men huddled by the hearth. The girls clustered around Lizzie, touching her ring and listening to her describe her future wedding. Hazel's eyes sparkled, and she wrapped an arm around my waist.

"Appears that you and Charlie might be next," she whispered. "Has he asked you?"

"No." I slipped from her grasp. Her words both warmed and pricked my heart.

"I heard that," Janie said. "Reckon they both be needing more time. Viney's finally coming to her senses. Charlie's still settling in."

At that moment Charlie and Seamus pushed open the door. They stamped their heavy boots, and I rushed to greet them. Charlie handed me a poke smelling like oranges.

"I thought your guests might like some fruit. Make certain that you save a few for you and Jacob." Charlie hung his coat on a peg.

"Thank you." I inhaled the pungent citrus scent.

"Please, Viney. Please." Children circled me, reaching with chapped hands.

"I'm a-going to fill up a bowl and set these with the other vittles. You biggest ones take an orange to your mamas and have her peel sections for each of you. Share now." Like a swarm of yellow jackets seeking sweetness, the children snatched the oranges.

Seamus and Jacob began fiddling "Whiskey Before Breakfast," and Mr. Lloyd played along on his banjo. Folks started clogging, and Lizzie pulled Lucas to the center of the cabin. Queer, I thought, Lucas usually playacted with the mummers who would arrive in a bit. And if a girl jilted me, I'd not dance with her. My eyes searched for Charlie.

He fumbled with a pair of wooden bones, trying to click and clack them to the reel's rhythm. My feet shuffled as I moved toward him.

"Shove those in your pocket. Join in." I grabbed his free hand.

He pulled back. "If I cannot accompany this beat with my fingers, how could I ever manage that footwork?"

"I tried your prissy dances. 'Bout made a fool of myself."

Charlie's eyes snapped. My feet rocking beneath me, I bobbed up and down before him.

"Think: shuffle, step, rock, step. Keep changing feet. Dare you." I took his hand, and we danced over by Seamus. He grinned.

"On with ye, now."

"Shuffle, step, rock, step," Charlie muttered, watching his feet.

"Don't look down. 'Tis easier if'n you feel the beat." I closed my eyes and let the reel ripple through me.

"Impossible. An Englishman guards his emotions."

"Tonight loosen your feet. And your feelings."

I watched Charlie's face through half-closed eyes. Finally, his shoulders relaxed a mite and his feet glided into the shuffles. I cut loose with a buck-'n-wing. Charlie tried to mimic me, but his feet stumbled. He reached for me with both hands on my waist, and we twirled round and round as Seamus and Jacob raced through "I Love Somebody, Yes, I Do."

Suddenly, Seamus flew off into an Irish reel, and his notes soared like a comet. Dozens of notes shimmered and pulsed through the room. Seamus's feet commenced slapping the floor, like our clogging, but stiffer. Folks clapped and cheered. Sweat ran down his temples. He slid into a modal tune and ended with his bow hitting each note three times.

I stared at Seamus's hands. How did his fingers wing across those strings? And Seamus knew a passel of those sad, slow tunes I had heard him play each night when I stayed at the Hills'. Did he make up tunes like I drafted weaving patterns? I'd had to shove my loom into a corner to make room for this frolic, but hearing those tunes made my fingers itch to weave. Tomorrow I would finish that coverlet.

Someone banged on the door and shouted:

"Open the door and let us in!
We come your favor for to win.
We shall sport and we shall fight.
And we shall act for you tonight."

The mummers! I wondered where they had hid.

"Time for playacting," Jacob called, and set down his fiddle.

Lizzie opened the door, and a cluster of lads marched in wearing sacks over their heads. The eye slits were rimmed with black, and different colored hair had been painted on each sack. One lad wore an old nightdress with an apron, another ripped overalls, and another a Confederate soldier's jacket.

"You've seen mummers before?" I asked. Charlie still breathed hard, and had rolled up his sleeves. I liked the golden red color of the hair on his forearms, like a fall sunset on a field of fodder shocks.

"Yes, I acted in our village play."

One of the mummers bawled:

"Make room and clear the way!
Make some room to see our play!"

Everyone moved back as the boy in overalls pranced about the center of the room.

"Looky here at this big fish! Stew it for dinner, old woman! Boil it in a big pot!" He pretended to throw the fish at Lizzie, and she squealed.

"I'll do no such thing. Can't abide fish stew. Fried it will be." The old woman said in a high voice. She shook a frying pan at her husband.

"Stewed." The old man hit her backside with the fish.

"Fried!" She mocked a wallop to his head with her pan, and he tumbled to the floor. Another mummer dashed over and examined the man.

"Call a doctor!" he shouted. "The old man needs a doctor!"

"Make way for a doctor!" someone in the crowd called as the lad in the Confederate coat knelt down.

"He don't need no doctor for healing," the old woman said. "Just a kiss from a fair maid."

"A kiss! A kiss!" the crowd shouted. I found myself being pushed to the front alongside Lizzie and Janie. Lizzie acted bashful-like as the old woman sashayed toward her.

"Pucker up! Who'll be this year?" the old woman asked, and pinched Lizzie's cheek. "Such a comely lass."

No mountain boy said *comely lass*. I recognized that

voice and looked down at polished boots. I glanced at the old man. He wore fine leather, too.

"Place your lips on his, lovey," the mummer crooned to Lizzie. For certain, he was Robert.

Lizzie hadn't done a thing to help get ready for the party. How dare she invite these foreigners to my cabin. I'd show them!

I shoved Lizzie aside and ran to the old man. The shaving stink gagged me as I leaned over him and smacked my lips against his. George drew me in closer, his tongue pushing apart my lips. As he tried to tangle his tongue with mine I bit him. His eyes popped open. Lizzie's hands pinched me as she pulled me off.

"Get away from him!"

"You're engaged," I said. "Almost married. Ain't fitting to kiss this fellar."

"Hit's George, and you knew it!"

George flung off his mask and leaped up. He glared at me. The other lads removed their costumes.

"Can't outfox Viney." Janie said.

"Feisty and muleheaded," Lucas added. Folks laughed and snickered.

"Are you certain that you want this vixen for a sister-in-law?" Robert nudged George. Whiskey fouled Robert's breath. "She needs taming."

"Play party time!" Jacob called, and frowned at me. "Name a singing game!"

"Over the River to Charlie!" Lizzie shouted out, and grabbed Charlie's hand. Jacob joined her, with Hazel.

My heart lurched at the sight of my sister gazing up at

Charlie and squeezing his hand. Suddenly, Robert gripped my fingers and led me into the longways set. I'd have walked away, but I knew Jacob was already riled over me giving folks something to wag their tongues on.

Lizzie began to sing:

"Charlie's sweet and Charlie's neat,
Charlie he's a dandy,
Charlie he's the very lad,
Who stole my striped candy."

"If you are so eager for kissing, I'm available." Robert spilled the hot words into my ear. His hands burned mine each time he turned me.

"And if'n I did, I'd puke on your boots," I snapped, and pulled away. Robert only laughed.

"Grand right and left," Jacob reminded everyone.

Right hand. Left hand. Men and women wove the two rings into one. Anger danced in Charlie's eyes when we glided past each other. Was he mad at Robert for dancing with me or at me for kissing George?

"Swing your own!" Jacob called, and caught up Hazel.

Robert's thumb dug into my back as we whirled around. I tried to free my fingers, but he clenched my hand and pressed me closer. The whiskey clung to his words and watered my eyes.

"You're wasting your time with Charlie. Or is it the Paddy? I can dress you finer than Lizzie. Silks. Satins. I'd like to see your hair tumbling over bare shoulders. Trade that rag for a gown like Lizzie wore New Year's Eve."

"I wove this dress." I gritted my teeth and heaved. "With my own hands."

"Ah, such sweet hands." Robert staggered, caught himself, and reached for me. A pair of hands thrusted him aside, and Robert stumbled back against my loom.

"Kindly leave Miss Viney alone. The dance is over, I believe," Charlie said.

Robert stood a few inches taller than Charlie, but farm work had hardened Charlie's muscles. Robert couldn't beat him.

"Well, inform me when you tire of bringing that wench to your stables. I've the silver to reward her for pleasuring me."

"How dare you speak of Viney like that!" Charlie said.

I blanched. "Don't." I caught Charlie's arm as he aimed his fist. "Folks will gossip enough about tonight's doings. Anyway, his kind isn't worth the powder to blow them to hell." I glared at Robert. If I'd had a hoe, I would have lit into him myself.

"As you wish." Charlie shook me off and strode over to Seamus.

Other folks passed looks back and forth. A tired toddler cried. Woman gathered plates and cups into baskets.

"Good-bye!" our neighbors called as they hefted children to their shoulders. "Thank ye for the fine time."

They left in clusters, with most men armed. Sam had said that panther had been near his barn two nights ago. Jacob rode off on Barney with Hazel in front of him. Lizzie marched away between Robert and George.

"One of those fellars should be toting a gun," I said.

"Aunt Alta heard the panther last night." I studied Seamus and Charlie. "Y'all should have one, too."

"I'll play me fiddle and lull him to sleep," Seamus said.

"Thank you for inviting me." Charlie held my hands in his. His eyes scanned my face. He lifted one hand and kissed it. "Good night."

I thrust that hand in my pocket, still feeling Charlie's lips. The look in his eyes made me feel guilty. My plan to befriend him so as to hush folk's gossip about staying single seemed to be working. What would I do if he did fancy me? I shivered on the porch watching the lads duck under snow-laden pine branches and step up the path. Thin clouds skimmed the sky. A ring circled the waning moon. Such a ring meant snow was coming. The air on the porch still smelled of pipe tobacco. As I pushed open the door a scream sliced the stillness.

Panther! And Jacob off. I glanced around the cabin. My lovesick brother had left his gun. Another scream rippled through the darkness. My fingers trembled as I loaded the gun and dashed out.

My feet slid on the packed snow covering the trail. Branches snagged my hair and skirts. My lungs burned. Shouting rumbled from up ahead. I crested a rise and saw Lizzie. She screamed and pointed.

Bodies thundered and rolled toward the Clear Fork. Fallen branches snapped. Men grunted and cursed. I tried to remember what Jacob had taught me about shooting.

"Where's the panther? Did it jump them?" I squinted through the underbrush for a tawny shape. "Tell me where to aim."

"Don't!" Lizzie grabbed my arm. "Ain't no panther! Charlie jumped Robert. George downed Seamus. They'll roll over the ledge if'n we don't stop 'em. Crash into the river. All them rocks."

"Hurry!" I slid down the slope, fighting my skirts and the brush. The rush of the river rose from below. Lizzie stumbled after me.

"DO SOMETHING!" Lizzie screamed.

I dug my boots into the snow and lifted the gun toward the sky. The blast jolted me back, and I tasted black powder. The shot rolled between the hills.

Kathunk! They must have hit something. The cursing stopped.

Out of the gloom a tall figure staggered toward me. Robert! He paused, picked up something, and cackled. Three other figures struggled up the hill. Robert's eyes met mine, and he grinned.

"He said he was defending *your* honor." Robert swayed and spat blood. I recognized the cloth bag in Robert's hand. Seamus fiddle clicked against the bow.

"Your Paddy's fiddle, isn't it? I hate its screeching." Robert whirled around and swung.

"NO!" I threw myself upon him, but only added weight to the blow. Wood smashed. Strings twanged. Slivers sliced the cloth bag and pierced the snow. Charlie and Seamus ran toward us.

"Me fiddle!" Seamus sank into the churned up snow snatching at the fragments.

I wanted to die.

"See what you started!" Lizzie screamed at me. "Messing

with George!" She shoved me aside and flung herself onto George. "Get me out of here."

Clutching his shoulder, Charlie stumbled over to Seamus and knelt next to him. I wanted to join them, but my feet were stones.

The cold metal of the gun sank into my hands. This was my fault. Charlie had fought on account of me. Seamus lost his fiddle because of my foolishness.

George, Robert, and Lizzie plodded up the path, heading to Rugby.

"Come home with me," I said to Charlie and Seamus. Tears chilled my cheeks. "Please." I touched Charlie's hands.

Seamus clutched his cloth bag. Charlie tramped beside me. We met Jacob riding in on Barney as we entered the clearing. He shook his head as Charlie told what had happened.

"You'uns ride Barney over to the Hills'. Seamus take the reins. And *you*." He glowered down at me. "You get in that cabin."

I stumbled inside and threw off my clothes. Sliding between icy sheets, I wept. I would never be able to right all this.

Chapter Fifteen

*Thus a rift is set between the sexes at babyhood that
widens with the passing of the years.*

EMMA BELL MILES, *The Spirit of the Mountains*

*J*acob's words didn't keep me to the cabin, but the shame
in my heart did. The next morning Jacob learned that Charlie
and Seamus stayed on at the Hills'. The lads were banished
from the settlement for a time to allow tempers to cool. When
Jacob told me that Charlie had broken his shoulder, I went
out and split kindling until I wept. The crack of the wood
sounded like Seamus's fiddle hitting the tree, driving into me
what I had done last night. I lifted my hatchet, reflecting on
my muleheaded ways.

If my ma had lived, would her hands have gentled me?
I didn't blame Pa for walking away and leaving the aunts to
raise Lizzie and me. Aunt Idy had always shaken her head
and said, "Chancellorsville done it. After hearing those big
cannons, your pa never was the same." The roar of battle still
echoed in his mind, pushing out thoughts about his daughters. My aunts had done right by us, teaching us the manners
expected of women.

Why did *I* question what they taught us? Other girls

didn't balk at eating after the men or marrying at fifteen. With a babe on their hip, they hoed and churned even when their bellies swelled with another young'un. But those girls must not have that itch to weave the sight of the light through the leaves into coverlets. They considered working with their hands merely a part of their daily portion, not something that could stir their hearts. I swiped my apron across my face. If I hadn't playacted about courting, Charlie wouldn't have jumped Robert.

Jacob paid no mind to my red eyes and nose. Most days he was off hunting or tanning deer hides, which he tacked to the sides of our barn. I pondered the notion of speaking to Aunt Idy, but in the aunts' one-room cabin there was no privacy. I *knew* what Aunt Alta would say it was high time I get shut of my willful, foolish spirit and settle into the harness God made for women.

Days slipped into weeks. I came to admit that I missed those lads. I wanted to hear Charlie name the clouds and talk about his barometer. I yearned to hear Seamus play his fiddle. Thinking about his broken fiddle drove me back to splitting kindling. Somehow I had to make up for what I had destroyed.

A little tufted-bird was singing "Peter, Peter" one February afternoon when Mrs. Hill came to call. She hung her felted bonnet on a peg and stood warming her hands by the fire while I brewed tea.

"I thought you might enjoy the new book Amos bought me, called *Little Men*. By the same author who wrote *Little Women*."

"Thank you, ma'am. I appreciate your kindness," I said.

Mrs. Hill smiled at me in that thoughtful way I loved. She spoke nary a word about Seamus and Charlie, and didn't let on if Lizzie had told on me.

"Have you completed all the weaving you planned?" she asked. "Designed any new patterns?"

Such gentleness tugged at my innards. My eyes filled. I licked my lips.

"Been working steady." My voice trembled. My eyes pooled.

"What is it child?" Mrs. Hill placed her hand on mine.

"Everything!" I spilled it all out. Notching the axle. The snake. Kissing George to rile Lizzie, the boys' fight. Throwing myself on Robert as he smashed the fiddle into the tree.

"I'm so confused. I don't want to be some twitter-witted gal, but why can't I be like other girls and still stay me. Why did Lizzie have to change into a snooty lady? Why did those foreigners come here and mess with our lives?" I kept sobbing, gulping down air, and blowing my nose on my apron. Finally Mrs. Hill gave me her lace-edged hankie, took me in her arms, and rocked me like I was a least one.

"Oh, dear, dear," she repeated. When the flood ended, she released me. "I wondered when you would confess about the incidents at the Opening."

"You knew?" I snuffled my nose. "From Lizzie?"

"Yes, but *only* after I asked her. When you kept avoiding me, I figured you were guilty, then I spoke with Lizzie."

"What are you fixin' to do with me?"

"Perhaps the proper question is what *you* should do to make things right?"

"I'm sorry about the snake, ma'am, and I reckon I

should pay for the axle. Could Mr. Hill subtract the cost from what's left of our credit at the commissary?" I sat up a bit straighter and tried to smooth the crushed spots on my apron where I had blown my nose.

"The snake, well, any lad might have pulled such a prank. The axle *could* have caused serious mischief if the horses had been trotting, but in all that mud . . . I'll speak to Mr. Hill. He'll withdraw the price from your account and extend some credit that you can work off."

"Thank you, ma'am. But I still can't abide what these foreigners are doing. I want to be shut of them and their town. Streets slicing the forest. Houses sprouting everywhere. I thought these foreigners came to farm." I tried to keep my voice level and low.

"I can understand some of your feelings about the town, but Mr. Hill did encourage the men to leave as many trees as they could around the Tabard. I don't think you can change what has happened. The English press has declared that Rugby is a place that all well-educated young people should experience. This summer we expect many visitors, and some will decide to settle here. Do remember, dear, that Mr. Hill and I were once foreigners."

"But you're different! Built yourselves a little cabin and farm. Didn't lumber your woods. Live mostly like us."

"Yes, I suppose we do seem different from these recent arrivals. But after fighting in the War Between the States, Mr. Hill only wanted a quiet life. The same as Charlie and Seamus do."

Their names slid between us like when I stepped on a treadle and sent a full shuttle flying through the warp's web.

I poked at the fire and tossed on a log. My eyes followed the rush of sparks up the chimney.

"How's Charlie's shoulder, ma'am? And Seamus?"

"Charlie's shoulder is mending well. And Seamus, he burned the wreckage of his fiddle. It and the bow could not be repaired. Without music Seamus is . . ." She sighed.

I knew it. It would be the same as if my wheel and loom were snatched from me.

"What can I do, ma'am? I have to *do* something!"

"First, you must stop using those lads."

I stared at her. My stomach sank lower and lower, past my knees, into my toes.

"Lizzie and I suspected you're flirting with the lads so that folks will assume you are courting. I am confused as to why you are playacting. You've criticized Lizzie so often for using men, but how are your actions any different?"

I was no better than Lizzie, who *had* tried to warn me. And the lady I admired the most had rubbed the sleep from my eyes. My heartbeat drummed in my forehead, beating Mrs. Hill's words into my brain.

"I didn't mean any harm . . . I just wanted folks to stop nagging on me about marrying." Tears wet my cheeks. What sort of person had I become?

"You have a good heart, Viney. Show that to Charlie and Seamus. If you only want to be friends, tell them that. But first, ponder if you are being honest with yourself."

"Yes, ma'am." I wiped my eyes. Only the look on Seamus's face that horrible night had hurt as badly as Mrs. Hill's rebuke. Shame squeezed me. "I've been thinking. I *have* to buy Seamus another fiddle. I finished the coverlets for Mr.

Foster, along with two others. Could the inn buy those two? How soon can I send Mr. Foster his coverlets?"

"Mr. Hill can take the order to Sedgemore in a few weeks, after the roads dry. As for the inn, they won't need any more bed linens until closer to June, and at this time, they would prefer to trade."

"Yes, ma'am. Is there any person at the inn who'd pay for the coverlets? I must buy that fiddle."

"You could ask Miss Ringgold. She spoke to me once about your weavings."

My mind showed me Miss Ringgold's jeweled hand joining Lizzie's hand with George's. And Miss Ringgold's look of distain when my hair tumbled. She'd been the first to criticize Charlie's green ribbon and to say I dressed like a servant.

"Isn't there anyone else, ma'am?"

"I don't think so. Did you know that Miss Ringgold is Robert's sister?"

"No, ma'am." I would never go to that girl. *Never.* I'd go wild crafting, gathering healing plants. I would earn what I needed from my hills.

Mrs. Hill tied on her bonnet and fastened her shawl. "Listen to your heart. You're a good lass." She kissed my cheek.

Mrs. Hill's words had thawed my grief, and I was determined to make her proud of me.

Spring refused to come. I'd hoped to dig ginseng by late February, but cold nights drove the frost deeper into the earth. Come March, I tramped the woods with a shovel and basket, but the heavy snows had flattened last summer's undergrowth. Even though I knew where large patches of ginseng grew, others had dug there last fall. I only took a few roots, and they dried into a puny pile.

Like a bad chigger bite, a voice kept whispering to me that I should try to sell those coverlets to Miss Ringgold. Only a few minutes of sweet-talking and smiling and I would hold her cash money. It's your pride that's keeping you poor, that voice goaded. Finally a head cold latched the door on my wild crafting. I hunkered down by the fire and read Mrs. Hill's book about wild boys living with Jo and Professor Baer. Those lads put me in mind of Charlie and Seamus throwing peaches at Royal Robert and King George.

One March morning Charlie rode in and tied Mr. Hill's horse to a sapling by the barn. His shoulder moved freely beneath his woolen jacket when he shook Jacob's hand. Wind-chapped and ruddy, Charlie resembled Jacob more than that lad who had trudged along the ridge road a year ago. I heard the sheep bawling as the menfolk set to shearing. My feet wanted to run and help, but I felt shy.

"Best run your fingers through your hair," Jacob warned Charlie as they walked through the door at noon. "Shouldn't be no ticks, but can't never tell." The two of them removed their boots and coats and hung them on the porch.

After dinner I set mugs of mint tea and a dried apple pie before them. Our cracked mugs appeared pitiful compared to Mrs. Hill's china. Charlie spooned honey into his tea and looked at me through the tea's steam.

"I'm sorry we've no milk. Cindy Lou freshens in April," I said, and cut the pie.

"This is fine. It will take the chill off." Charlie picked up his fork.

Jacob inhaled one piece of pie and scooped up a second.

"Need to have you come over more," Jacob said. "Ain't seen pie since Old Christmas."

I could have strangled my brother, and tried to kick him under the table. Charlie simply stirred his tea.

"Heard that Land Board of yourn's untangled themselves. Goin' to sell land soon."

"Yes," Charlie answered. "They're opening up the sale of several hundred acres. Seamus and I hope to buy a small section, but prices keep rising. More settlers are arriving as the roads clear, and they have similar aspirations."

"And your pa?" I hadn't forgotten Charlie's father's demands.

"He hasn't changed his mind. Either I plow my own land this spring, or I must leave in late April."

"Sorry to hear that," Jacob said. "You're turning into a fine farmer." He dragged his sleeve across his mouth. "You sit here a spell and cheer Viney. Sorriest gal these past weeks."

I'd have liked to die after Jacob's words. He clattered off, leaving Charlie and me with only the snap of the fire speaking.

"Is there more tea?" Charlie asked.

"Yes. I'm sorry." I filled his mug. Seemed all I could do was beg his pardon, but the apology that needed to come choked me.

"How's Seamus?" I watched Charlie's face.

"Glum." Pain and anger rose into his eyes. "Speaking of leaving."

"Leaving!" I slumped into my chair. "Why? No pa forcing him home, is there? Y'all can't both leave me."

"I thought you wanted all us foreigners to leave the ridge?" Charlie stared at his tea.

"Well, Robert and his kind should pack up today and take that sawmill with them. But I'm not wanting you and Seamus to leave."

"And whose departure would hurt you the most?" Charlie whispered. "Seamus or myself?" His knuckles whitened as he clutched his mug.

"Don't. Please don't ask such a question." Tears rose into my eyes as I traced the grain of the wood along the tabletop.

"Viney."

I had to look up at Charlie. He leaned forward and took one of my hands.

"Your answer is important." He brushed his thumb against my palm.

Mrs. Hill's reprimand rattled through me. I felt as if I was wearing one of Lizzie's corsets, and couldn't breathe.

"I'm sorry about your shoulder, about Seamus's fiddle. Sorry I made as if we were courting. Flirting." My eyes puddled. "I want to make it right. I do. Buy Seamus a fiddle and bow."

"And me?" Charlie asked.

"I want to do right by you, too! You're the best friend I ever had."

"Friend?" Charlie withdrew his hand. "I was hoping . . ."

"I . . . I . . ." How could I tell Charlie that I didn't *know* what I felt or what I wanted? I commenced weeping, seemed to be a habit these days. Charlie offered me his handkerchief.

"It's clean." Same words he used that storm-filled night.

"Thank you." I blew my nose and sat twisting the piece of linen. If I was to keep up this crying, I should hem me some of these snot-rags. Charlie picked up the copy of *Little Men*.

"Did you know that we're starting to build a free library? It's to be for your people, too. The opening day is planned for June. Mr. Hughes will be back. I hope I'm still here for that day."

"I hope you are, too." I bit my lip and smiled. "I honestly mean that."

"I should be going." Charlie pushed in his chair.

"Your handkerchief?" I squeezed the crumpled linen.

"Keep it. I've been thinking of purchasing a new fiddle for Seamus. A parting gift. Mr. Hill said he'd order one when he took the wool to Knoxville."

"But you're saving for land!"

"Yes." Charlie shrugged.

"When's Mr. Hill fixin' to travel?" I clenched the wadded linen.

"Day after tomorrow." Charlie slipped on his hat and coat, and shut the door behind him.

After Charlie left, I wandered out to the barn, where Jacob was messing with his plow. If only I had the cash money from those Cincinnati coverlets, I'd buy Seamus's fiddle. I sat down on a pile of straw.

"Kiss and make up?" Jacob asked as he tightened a bolt.

"Jacob! We're only friends!" I stuffed Charlie's handkerchief into my pocket.

"Sure. That fellar rides over, alone, to shear your sheep. Asks a passel of questions about you. Hintin' at being asked into the cabin. I thought you fancied the lad."

"Well, I don't know." I picked up a handful of hay and fed it to Cindy Lou.

"Don't know! Stop acting so dim-witted."

"I don't need any man tellin' me what to do!" I inched toward the barn door, but Jacob caught my arm.

"Sit! You a-gonna listen. Charlie's a fine man. And so is Seamus, if he's the one you fancy. They're both honorable fellars who'd be good husbands. If'n you'd pull the wool out of your head, you'd see that."

I was shaking, but I didn't know if it was from anger or shame. I started to rise, but Jacob towered over me.

"Not yet. You best be thinking a few years ahead. Who's gonna sit by the fire with you on a winter's night when Lizzie's in England and Hazel and I are wed? You've scared away every fellar on the ridge."

"Don't care." I tried to focus my hearing on Cindy Lou chewing her cud.

"Should care. Can't you see what I'm coming to? You're too queer for ridge fellars."

"Right about that. Leeches, all of them. Sucking the life from their women."

"Viney! Shut your mouth." Jacob sat down next to me. "You need a man who's not set in his ways. Someone who will love you because you *have* to be weavin'."

"Charlie? But his pa's calling him home."

"I have a notion that he'd work harder at staying if'n you gave him a reason."

"Jacob." I squeezed my eyes shut so tightly, my ears hummed. "May I please borrow Barney tomorrow morning?" I let out my breath and glanced at him.

"Laws! All this speechifying worked a miracle. You went and asked nicely." He grinned. "Or maybe it was sitting with Charlie?"

"Oh, stop it!" I knocked his hat in the water trough and bolted for the cabin.

CHAPTER SIXTEEN

She [a mountain woman] *was not filled with a vain*
longing for unknown paths, but with an intense
delight in the one she was traveling.

FRANCES GOODRICH, *Mountain Homespun*

Next morning after Jacob lit out to split rails, I wrapped the two unspoken-for coverlets in a piece of muslin. Tomorrow Mr. Hill would ride off to Knoxville, so I had only today to earn cash. I buttoned up my blue-checked dress, even though the cuffs were fraying. I'd been so busy weaving coverlets, I'd not sewn any new dresses this winter. Some of the threads in the skirt had been pulled by briars that awful night, and I tried to smooth out the snags.

I kicked my heels and made Barney trot. "We'll take our time coming home." I knew I had to nippity-tuck it to the settlement before I lost my grit and turned back. Two strange boys met me at the stable and tied Barney to a post. Pained me not to see Charlie's barometer hanging in the barn.

Lizzie stared at me when I opened the kitchen door. She stood on a little ladder. Her ring flashed as she stacked dishes on the higher shelves. Her dark green calico swayed with the movement of her crinolines, like oak leaves in a breeze.

"Mercy! Is something amiss with Jacob? Or the aunties?"

"No. I came to town. I didn't think you worked here now."

Lizzie's hands paused. "Do tell! And where did you think I was working?"

"I thought George . . . He being so rich . . . he'd pay for you to stay here. You wouldn't need to work in the kitchen."

Lizzie turned red and nearly tumbled off the ladder. She marched over and planted herself in front of me.

"My own sister! Is that what you think of me?" Her silver locket swung back and forth. "Do you think Jacob would tolerate such?" She backed me against the trestle table.

I tried to push her away, but her broad skirt hemmed me in. What in tarnation had I done to have both Jacob and Lizzie fly at me? "Leave off! Just tell me where I can find Miss Ringgold?"

"Why?" Lizzie sucked in air, fighting her corset. "What do you want with my friend?"

I about snapped, Ain't for you to know, but checked my tongue. "Mrs. Hill sent me."

Lizzie's shoulders relaxed. "She's in the parlor, off the west room. Having a late breakfast."

I dodged around Lizzie's bustle and dashed through the swinging door. I'd worn my boots and paused to brush the dirt off the toes. Voices murmured behind the French doors. I knocked.

"Enter," Miss Ringgold said in her chiseled accent.

I shoved open the door and spied Miss Ringgold and Royal Robert sitting near a window. A familiar ostrich fern left over from Opening Day brushed her chair. Eggs sat in squatty candleholders on the table, along with plates of biscuits and toast with melted butter. Robert set down his newspaper, and his eyes swept over me. I wanted to bolt.

"Yes?" he said.

"I've come to see your sister."

They exchanged glances.

"Yes?" she said.

I marched to her side and opened my bundle. "Mrs. Hill said you might be interested in buying these coverlets. She thought you'd like them as a remembrance of your time in the mountains."

Miss Ringgold wrinkled her nose and fingered the weavings. "You dyed the wool with some plant?"

"Yes, miss." I gagged out the title. "Used pokeberry set with vinegar."

"Set?" She shoved the coverlet away and held a lavender-scented hanky to her long nose.

"Vinegar sets the dye. Makes it lasting. After a time, this color will fade to the reddish orange of autumn leaves." I knew by her look that she wouldn't buy my weaving. I hated how I had lowered myself, but I *had* to find a buyer. I swallowed the bile rising in my throat.

"If you're not interested, miss, do you know someone who might be?"

"No." Miss Ringgold picked up her silver spoon and tapped at her egg like a woodpecker. I stuffed the coverlets in the muslin and ran toward the door.

"Stop." Robert commanded. "You have not shown *me* the blankets."

Hell can freeze over before I sell you my weavings was

what I longed to say. But my fingernails snagged on one of my dress's pulled threads, reminding me of the twang of the fiddle strings as they snapped. I stomped over to Robert.

"No," he ordered. "Drape them over the settee."

Biting my lip, I did as Robert ordered, feeling his eyes following my backside.

"Very pretty. Bring that one here." He pointed. "I want to examine it more closely."

"Oh, Robert! Make up your mind!" Miss Ringgold said. "That stench makes my head ache."

"The smell will recede?" Robert glanced at the small slips of paper pinned to the fabric, where I'd written eight dollars.

"Yes, sir. Just hang it in the fresh air for a day." I feared the prices were too high, but Robert smirked as he fished out a silver clip filled with bills. I held out my hand.

He paused. "Perhaps you should do that for me? I will ride out at the end of the week and pick them up." He began pocketing the bills.

"But please." I choked on the words. "If'n you don't mind,"—I held out my hand—"I'd like to be paid today." How I wished I was throwing peaches at this rogue instead of begging.

"I'll pay you when I come out. On Friday."

"Then I'll look elsewhere." I folded up the other coverlet, hating myself for groveling for money. There had to be some other way to earn cash.

Robert strode next to me. "Here." He held out several bills, his arm brushing against my shoulder. "Take them."

I ripped them from his fingers and threw open the French doors.

"Friday," Robert called. "And that's more money than those two are worth. Use the extra I provided to buy some cloth. I'd like to find you in a respectable frock."

I dashed out of the inn and onto the veranda. Gazing at the wispy clouds, I gulped down air. I preferred the acrid smell of pokeberry to Robert's bay rum. Why had I allowed him to order me about? To invite himself to *my* cabin? How much more had he given me? I opened my hand and stared at two ten-dollar bills. Before the settlers came, this could have bought ten acres of land. Did the fool think he could buy me with the extra four dollars? If not for Seamus, I'd slap the bills back into Robert's face.

Out of the corner of my eye, I saw Mr. Hill walking toward the commissary. Clutching my weavings, I ran across the road and up the street where goldenseal had once grown.

"Mr. Hill!"

Mr. Hill smiled and paused. "Good morning. Delivering an order?"

"Good morning, sir. Yes. Please. Could you buy a fiddle for Seamus when you're in Knoxville?" I held out the bills. "I've cash."

"Great heavens! You could purchase two, maybe even three fiddles with that sum!" Mr. Hill extracted a ten-dollar bill. "I'll bring you the change when I return."

"Thank you, sir. And please don't tell Seamus. It's a surprise." My cheeks flushed.

"Certainly. And take care of that cash. With today's land sale, there are many newcomers about town." Mr. Hill nodded toward the Land Board's office. "Door's to open in a few minutes."

A crowd of men pressed against the Land Board's door. I recognized Seamus, but most were foreigners dressed in corduroy and tweed. A few mountain men in their patched broadfalls stood apart, watching the doings. I walked over to Seamus.

"Where's Charlie? Are you two aiming to buy?"

"He's inside that knot of men. Door opens in one minute."

A gent in a frock coat stood in the office window with a gold watch open in his hand.

"Do y'all have enough cash?" I asked.

"We'll soon know." Seamus answered. "But some parcels are as high as twenty dollars an acre."

"Here." Without thinking, I pressed my ten-dollar bill into his palm. "Push in there."

Seamus stared at the cash money. "Miss Viney, no. We can't." The door lock rattled.

"You will. Every bit helps. Find Charlie." I shoved Seamus into the throng. Men elbowed each other, shouting and waving bills. I stepped back, afraid my skirts would drag me in with the crowd. I wasn't certain why I had given away the last of my earnings, but I had a peace about doing it.

"You fixin' to buy, Viney?" Abel Campbell called. "Or gonna marry one of them gents?"

I glared at Abel. "What I do is none of your business." I marched over to the commissary and hoped the lads would look for me there.

Running my hands across the bolts of chintz, muslin, and lawn soothed my mind. I counted the number of threads per inch, checked for twills, and wished I could watch them print calico. Mrs. Hill had told me about how artists etched patterns on copperplates. The plates were fitted onto rollers that ran over the fabric. I was fingering a sweet blue calico with yellow flowers when I heard Charlie's boots. His feet clomped in his own queer way.

"Fancy that one over the green?" Charlie asked. He took my hand and placed the ten-dollar bill into my palm.

I scanned his face. "What happened?"

"Too many men. Too few parcels available. Prices rose too high. More land is to open up for sale in June, but little good it will do me." Charlie sighed and stuffed his hands into his pockets.

"What will you do?" I wanted to kindle a light in his eyes, like when he spoke about the clouds.

"I'm not sure." He looked down at me. "Thank you for trying to help us."

I glanced to where Seamus stood looking at harmonicas. "I bought Seamus a fiddle," I whispered. "Mr. Hill's fetching it from Knoxville." My heart pounded in my ears. If Charlie knew who had given me the money, he'd be riled.

"He will be overjoyed." Charlie gazed at a display of tea and china cups. "May I assume by your loan that you would prefer that I remain in Rugby?"

"Yes. Truly." I knew I should say more, but my tongue felt starched.

"Then how about the blue calico *and* the green with roses? I'll buy one, and you purchase the other? You could use some new frocks."

Same words Robert had said. "Are you making fun of my dress? I wove this cloth with my own hands!"

"The most talented hands I know."

"But you're saving for land. And I couldn't be beholding . . . " I slid my hand over the smooth green calico, but my skin still prickled. A gent giving a girl ribbons or oranges was a small kindness, but to accept a dress would encourage the notion that I wanted to court.

"Perhaps we could trade. You could weave something small for my mother." His wistful smile and gentle words loosened something inside me. Jacob was right; Charlie was different from the men on the ridge.

"Thank you. I reckon we could do that."

"Good." Charlie took the coverlets from my arms and gave me the bolts of calico.

"Six yards," I said to the clerk, a new girl with gold curls licking her face. I eyed her neat dress with a ruffle. "Wait. How many yards to sew up a dress such as yours?"

"Eight, miss." Her voice told me she was a Yankee.

"I'll take eight."

Her scissors flashed through the fabric, slicing away a cloud of blue and a mist of green. Still carrying the weavings, Charlie took my arm and walked me to Barney. He loaded the saddlebags and helped me mount.

"Sunday's my only free day. Might I ride out?"

"Surely. We can choose a weaving draft for your mother. And I'll . . . bake you a pie." I clucked to Barney and waved good-bye. I would have to sew quickly to finish that green dress by Sunday. I felt like I was sucking on lemon drops, steeped in sweetness yet puckered by doubts. Courting would be the hardest pattern I had ever deciphered.

Chapter Seventeen

They do not understand that the semblance of prosperity
is only a temporary illusion that vanishes with
the departure of the summer people.

EMMA BELL MILES, *The Spirit of the Mountains*

All week it riled me to think on Royal Robert inviting himself to my cabin. Only way to stop him riding out was to return to Rugby, so Thursday afternoon I placed both coverlets into separate baskets and stepped out. Jacob was going to Hazel's for supper, so I had plenty of time.

I gazed up through the haze of baby green leaves and into the robin's-egg blue sky. Little black-and-white birds declared their territory, and other birds zipped by with nesting materials in their beaks. Was I ready to court a mate and build a nest? It pleasured me to think of Charlie riding up Sunday afternoon, but all that followed marriage made me want to slam a door and run deeper into the woods. Why couldn't I know my mind like Jacob and Hazel? I gripped my baskets and walked on.

As I was rounding the back of the inn I noticed Robert riding toward the stables, so I tramped to the wide doors, where a groom stood waiting for Robert's horse.

"Yes, miss?" the lad asked.

"I'm here to see him." I nodded my head at Robert as he dismounted. For a moment Robert stared at me.

"Right, miss. Please step aside. A load of hay is to arrive momentarily." The groom motioned to outside the doors. He reached for the reins to Robert's horse, but Robert shook his head.

"Here." Robert grabbed the boy's hand and pressed something in it. "I'll look after Diamond." He winked at the groom. "Sit in the shade and wait for that hay."

"Yes, sir!" the lad answered.

I tried to step away, but Robert gripped my shoulder with his free hand and shoved me ahead of him. The gray horse towered above me, and my baskets banged against my knees.

"Let me go!" I sputtered.

"How kind of you to chat with me while I brush down Diamond. He's been feisty today," Robert said in a loud voice. "This way, my dear." Robert's fingers dug into my flesh. "One sudden move and Diamond will kick. He was a devil all afternoon."

My skirts flapped as I struggled, and the horse's ears flicked back. The whites of his eyes glared down at me. I didn't dare struggle with the horse on my heels. Robert pulled me into stall and latched the door.

Get out! Get out, hammered in my head. But how? Robert released the reins, and Diamond snuffed in his empty manger. Robert rubbed the brute's flank.

"Easy, now. I'll see to your needs after a bit." Robert grinned at me. "How thoughtful of you to save me a trip to that despicable cabin. Or perhaps it is this barn that beckons you? Pleasant memories of Charlie in the hay mound?"

Robert moved closer, backing me into a corner. I watched the horse's hooves shift. The floorboards trembled under the stallion's weight and matched my quaking innards.

"Your mind's foul. Like you." I raised one basket.

"Feisty wench, aren't you." Robert caught my right arm as I threw the basket at his head. Diamond snorted and pranced.

"You she-devil!"

I tried to wallop him with the other basket, but he ducked.

"Didn't I tell you to dress decent for me?"

"Let me go!" I kicked at his boots.

I'd worn the old blue check to spite him, but as we fought, I heard the waist seam rip. A button popped off the front of the bodice. Robert grabbed my left arm and pressed me against the wall. Above our breathing, I heard the rattle of a wagon.

"The hay's comin'!" I could feel tears rising. I would not cry.

"I paid off the boy." Robert tightened his grip.

His lips traveled down my neck toward my open collar. I wanted to puke. Wheels crunched on the gravel. Who was driving that wagon? Arching my back, I twisted my left arm and thrust my basket into Robert's stomach. He fell backward. Diamond's rear end slammed the stall.

"When I get my hands on you . . ." Robert lunged for the halter, but missed.

"Help!" I screamed. "Wild horse!" I pressed myself into the corner away from Diamond's thrashing hooves, which separated me now from Robert.

"Where?" a voice shouted. Boots thundered across the floor.

"The last stall!" I screamed.

The bolt moved. Seamus grabbed Diamond's halter. I dashed out and tripped at his feet. Robert darted after me, grabbed my skirt, ripping it farther from the bodice.

"Miss Viney!" Seamus cried. "Merciful heavens!"

"Leave us alone, Paddy!" Robert shouted. "She took my money."

"For the weavings." I clutched my torn skirt. Another button had flown from the bodice. Inside the stall Diamond kicked one of the coverlets. My beautiful weavings trampled by that brute. Seamus stepped between Robert and me.

"Leave the lady alone." His eyes flicked over me with sadness.

"He paid me only for the coverlets." I began to cry. "He forced me into there."

"The devil I did," Robert said. "Only a slut visits a barn."

"Run to Janie. She'll tidy you up." Seamus pushed me toward the door. More boots stomped into the barn.

"Are you finished, Master Robert?" the groom called.

"For now," Robert answered, and strode off.

Sitting on Janie's bed, I wept. My elbows stuck out from my tattered sleeves. I stared at my swollen wrists. My bodice was half-open, exposing my chemise. What would wagging tongues say? How could I hush this?

"I'll kill him," I said. "I'll push him off a cliff. I'll . . . "

"He's a wicked boy, but not worth the sin of murder. He's made free with a couple of girls," Janie said. "Sweet-talked them. You were lucky. 'Sides, Robert and his snotty sister are fixin' to leave after Lizzie's wedding."

"Is that so? In the meantime, someone needs to tan his hide. I'll have Jacob tear him apart." I still shook and wanted to scrub away Robert's touch. I grabbed Janie's flannel washrag and lathered it with soap.

"I wouldn't tell Jacob. You did enter a barn with him. Even ridge folks would think you're willing. Why *did* you go? To make Charlie jealous?"

"O Laws! Is that what you think?"

"I think love's addled you. And that you don't know much about men. Or how young ladies should act."

I groaned. "What do you reckon Charlie will think?" I mopped up water I'd spilled. "What'll he do?"

"Either he'll bust open Mr. Robert's head, or he'll figure you was flirtin' with Robert."

"He wouldn't!"

"Might. Seeing you strung him along."

"But Charlie knows I can't stand Robert. I didn't want him coming to the cabin. That'd look like courting, too!"

Janie shrugged her shoulders. She handed me a soft brown calico dress. "Here, wear this. I'll find Seamus and talk to him. He'll explain everything to Charlie. You go home. I'll try and hush talk."

"Thank you." I slipped into Janie's dress. But I vowed

that before Robert sailed away, I'd get even. And I prayed that Charlie would believe Janie and Seamus.

A circuit rider came through on Sunday, and after the preaching I went home and waited in my new green calico. Charlie didn't come. Big black ants marched to the dried apple pie, so I kept brushing them off and moving the pie about the cabin. Finally I gave in and watched them suck at the sugary filling crusted along the pie's rim.

The day was soft and scented with the sweetness of spring. Jacob had walked off from meeting holding Hazel's hand. Janie and Sam had ridden back to her cabin on Sam's mule. I sat alone on the front porch with my cat on my lap, gazing across the ridge.

"Kitty, should I go on over to the Hills? See if Charlie is there?"

I could just imagine Aunt Alta shaking her head and fussing at me. "Good girls don't chase after fellars. They know *how* to draw the boys to them."

But in less than a month Charlie might leave! I had to find out what he was thinking. Who could I ask?

If only I could weave, I could beat out my troubles. But working on the Sabbath was a sin. Jumping up, I leaned against the porch railing, and the breeze flickered beneath my skirts. I hated this riled feeling. Just had to do *something*.

Serviceberry blossoms foamed among the trees, and I felt like I was slipping into a cloud as I lit into the woods. Clumps of bluets freckled shady patches, and swollen trillium buds hinted at the beauty to come. The earth was warm beneath my bare feet. I wandered toward the river. It would feel good to listen to the current rush around the rocks. I'd sit in the sun and watch minnows dart in little pools.

Up ahead, a girl giggled. Jacob and Hazel crested the path, their arms about each other's waists. I could feel threads snapping inside me. Janie and Sam. Jacob and Hazel. Lizzie and George. Coupling up.

"Viney!" Hazel called. "Want to join us?" Her sunbonnet had fallen back. Little blonde hairs had escaped from her braid, and they floated about her face like a halo. Jacob didn't take his arm away from her waist.

"No. Thinking about heading over to the Hills," I lied. Jacob gave me a funny look. Any fool could see I was walking the wrong way.

"Ain't there," Jacob said. "Saw them driving into town. Charlie and Seamus gone, too."

"Gone? Gone where?" I wiped my sweaty palms on my apron. Had Charlie left for good?

"Rode out to that buffalo cave over near Allardt. Lit out with a few others from the settlement."

"A few others?" I didn't mouth the real question: Were any girls with them?

"Mostly lads. Along with two English girls and that new gal who clerks at the commissary. Saw her riding next to Charlie, talking and laughing."

"Sure is a pretty day," Hazel said. "Come on with us, Viney. We're not far from my cabin." Though she spoke to me, her gray eyes shone up at Jacob. "I'll fix us something sweet to drink." Jacob looked like he was ready to kiss her any minute.

"No, thank you. I'll go on to the river. Water will cool

my feet." I didn't add that cooling off might be best for them, too.

"Bye," Hazel and Jacob said as they strolled around the bend.

I ambled to the river and pitched pebbles at a boulder, wishing it was Robert. All because of him, I was standing here alone.

"Don't care," I told a toad sitting beneath a slab of sandstone.

"Do too care," he seemed to croak as he hopped farther into the shade of the rock. "Do too."

CHAPTER EIGHTEEN

. . . we had heard . . . the sound of many axes and
crosscut saws, and, more often than was required
for the needs of my people, the crashing of
giant trees to the earth.

REBECCA CAUDILL, *My Appalachia*

On the first day of April, I stared at the skim of ice glazing a puddle. A north wind had swept in a blackberry winter for a few days. Was Charlie packing his trunk and fingering his ticket for England? I had finished the small weaving for his mother and should deliver it, but I couldn't bring myself to walk to the Hills.

Instead I unrolled the half-dozen weaving drafts left by my mother. Fingerprints smudged the edges of the papers. When I had turned twelve, Aunt Alta had brought a wooden box from the loft and opened it.

"These here were your ma's," she had said. "And if I recollect rightly, that one be your granny's writing. Appears you've been blessed with their gifts."

I pressed my thumb against one of the fingerprints. How old had my mother been when she wrote out this draft? Was she still unwed but in love with Pa? Or married and nursing Jacob? If she was here, I'd sit on the front porch and tell her of my trials. How I had playacted at courting but had only fooled myself. Was Janie right? Had I slip-slided into love? Was that why I grieved over Charlie not believing me?

Rolling up the drafts, I realized that I had stored only a few sketches of my own designs in the box. If I didn't write them out neatly, no far-off kin would be able to decipher my drafts. I could only find one sheet of paper. I smoothed it out and wrote: "Bright Spells and Showers." That's what Charlie called the days when the sun flickered between clouds that sprinkled the garden and moved on over the mountains. I set to marking the design I saw in my head, bits of light and dark. I reckoned that if Charlie had decided to sail home, I would give him a coverlet to remember me by. I tied up the harnesses so they matched my draft and commenced weaving. As I had no more paper to write out other drafts, I would have to visit either the Hills or the settlement.

A week passed before I borrowed Barney and rode over. The cold had melted away and the evening light lingered as a southern breeze tickled the treetops. Mr. Hill waved from where he was replacing fence posts in the pasture; Mrs. Hill was finishing up dishes.

"Welcome," Mrs. Hill said as she stacked china on a linen cloth.

"Howdy, ma'am. Need any help with the dishes?" I asked, and sniffed. Her kitchen smelled of ginger cookies.

"No, thank you. Just finished. Did you bring your knitting?"

"Yes, ma'am. And could I please borrow a few sheets of paper? I'll replace them the next time I visit the commissary."

"Think of the paper as a gift." Mrs. Hill pulled four sheets from Mr. Hill's desk. "Any special purpose for it?"

"Writing out weaving drafts of my designs, like my mama did."

"Ah, Aunt Alta told me a little about your parents. You never hear from your father?"

"Nary a word." I wondered what Mrs. Hill thought of a pa who ran away from his children.

"Such a pity. War alters men so. And I have something else for you. Came yesterday."

Mrs. Hill handed me a skinny slip of paper. "Bank of Cincinnati" was written in fancy letters at the top; underneath was my name.

"What is it, ma'am?"

"A bank check. Mr. Foster sent it as payment for your weavings."

"What a queer way to pay a person."

"You can use it like cash at the commissary. Mr. Foster also ordered five more coverlets for friends. Said they'd come by this summer for them. Now, how about tea and cookies on the porch? We'll knit and chat."

"Yes, ma'am." I carried out the cookies and sat on a rocker. We nibbled cookies for a few minutes while the tea steeped. This year's lambs raced for their mothers, bleating for a last bite before bedtime.

I rubbed my fingers over the rough linen paper of the bank check. No Walker had ever held such. I felt jittery, like when I drank a cup of coffee once with Aunt Idy. If I could continue earning money by weaving for city folks, never again would I stoop to begging cash from a cuss like Robert. Soon my ewe would lamb, and I'd have even more wool next spring. While Mrs. Hill poured me tea, I fit my toe into the dimple of a knothole.

"Mrs. Hill, . . . I was wondering . . . Did Charlie leave?" With my toenail I dug out a tiny bit of wool that had snagged on the ragged wood. "Haven't seen him in a spell."

"Mr. Hill and Charlie had many long talks. Finally Charlie wrote his father that he was staying on, but he has not received a reply. Charlie hopes that his father has not disowned him, but his decision means that he must work even harder now."

"At the settlement?"

"At the new sawmill. The lumber company brought in a bigger setup, so they hired extra hands."

"But he wants to farm! Why doesn't he work for you?"

"If Charlie and Seamus are going to buy land, they need to work at the highest-paying job they can find. Charlie no longer has that monthly allowance from home. Seamus never did. With the new sawmill the company needs more workers."

"But clearing the woods . . . " I slid down in my chair. "Does he ever talk of me?"

"These days Charlie is thinking more about buying a farm than young ladies. And perhaps he is confused about your affections." Mrs. Hill glanced sideways at me.

"It's that business with Robert!" I blushed.

"Yes. Neither lad could understand how you came to be in that stall. To them, just being with the horse was dangerous enough. Even Mr. Hill and I wonder why would you allow Robert to escort you into such a place?"

"Robert forced me!" I spat out the story, dropping stitches and splitting my yarn as I knitted too fast. "And if'n those boys won't believe the truth, then I'm finished with them!" I jammed my needles into the half-finished sock.

"Oh dear. Mr. Hill and I had heard gossip about Robert. I suppose since Robert is scheduled to leave soon, Mr. Hill decided to let things be. Give Charlie and Seamus time. With such a major decision to make, Charlie's mind's been elsewhere. And the lads are exhausted from the long days. I think if you show him that you care, then his eyes will gaze again at you. How are matters with Lizzie?" Mrs. Hill looked over at me.

"We aren't speaking."

"Well, I pray that you will talk to her. Her wedding is only three months away."

"George doing her right?"

"More than right. Mr. Hill and I pray that George's parents will be understanding."

"Ma'am?"

"George is breaking all the rules of English society. And even if his parents welcome Lizzie into the family, their friends may choose not to receive her. She will certainly miss home and need letters from her only sister."

"Serves Lizzie right if'n she misses home." I regretted my words when I saw Mrs. Hill sorrowful face. She set down her lacy knitting.

"Don't sow regret. Reconcile, please."

I stared out at the dim white of sheep dotting the darkening pasture. "I'll see. Best be off. Sun's about gone. Can I carry in your china?"

"No, thank you. You and Barney trot home."

"Night, ma'am." I picked up the rolls of paper.

"God bless."

Barney took me home in a skip and a hop. Jacob was still out sparking with Hazel. Moonlight shimmered across my loom when I entered the cabin. It highlighted the contrasting dark threads in the pattern I had designed especially for Charlie. Blast that boy! Reckon if Charlie wasn't leaving, then he didn't need any farewell present I picked up my scissors and sliced the warp. I would sew this sorry scrap into a pillow. Tomorrow I'd tie up these loose ends and commence with those five coverlets, weaving me more cash.

No matter how hard I worked, I missed Charlie. I planted and weeded my garden, but I kept looking at the sky and turning over the Latin names for the clouds. When I wore the green ribbon, I heard sleigh bells in my mind. Why had I thought I could mess with a man and not become as snarled as a burr in a fleece? I kept hoping one evening I'd hear the rattle of a wagon and find Charlie driving Mr. Hill's team.

I walked miles spinning more wool for the coverlets, trying to push Charlie out of my head. I dyed some of the yarn brown with walnuts and planned to color the other hanks with indigo. Jacob muttered when I gave him a bucket and asked him to carry it with him so he could collect his pee.

"I ain't taking it. You'll just have to save what you find in the chamber pot."

"If'n you don't oblige, this indigo pot's going to stink longer. Need more yellow water for it to brew quickly."

"I'll be glad when Hazel and I can wed! Be shut of you."

I'd known this announcement would come. "When's the wedding?" I focused on the greenish blue foam of the indigo pot. The raw smelling brew burned my nose.

"After the harvest."

I knew I should congratulate Jacob, but all I could think was where would I live? Jacob tugged my braid.

"Don't fret. You can stay on with us'n, if you like. Or you can move back in with the aunties."

"I'd die having to listen to Aunt Alta's tongue wag at me."

"Well, they are tickled to see you moping."

I scowled.

"I wish Lizzie was staying on for our wedding." Jacob picked up his hoe.

"When does she leave?"

"August. She's your only sister, Viney," Jacob said, and walked away. He didn't add, so make things right.

I glared at his back. Seemed like everyone I loved was shaking their fingers at me. I stomped off and weeded my garden.

The next afternoon I gave in. I blew the dust off the bank check and walked to the settlement. From far off, I heard the chug of the steam engine running the mill and the whine of the blade. I hated it and the stumps I passed. Canvas tents on platforms freckled the woods near rutted logging trails that twisted through the trees. A numbness spread over me. I couldn't stop this. Like a walnut brown dye seeping across a fleece, settlers and lumbermen continued to transform our ridge into their own world.

A team of horses pulling a load of logs came up a trail and toward me. Large chains encircled the logs and held them to the flatbed wagon. The air smelled of horses and leather. I closed my eyes and longed to return to the sweet forest that had grown here. A horsefly circled me, and I swatted.

"Steady," the driver said.

I backed up and squinted at Seamus. He jumped down and tied the reins to a tree. Taking my hands, he whirled me about.

"A mountain angel, ye are. Buying me that fiddle. A thousand thanks, Miss Viney. 'Tis even sweeter than my last. With a bow as nimble as your fingers. And that sturdy case."

"Had to do something. After that awful night—"

"No more on that," Seamus interrupted. "And such a long face you be wearing."

"Mrs. Hill said you and Charlie were lumbering." I looked at the sap oozing from the logs on the wagon.

"Needing every penny for the land we hope to buy. Charlie's at the mill. Dangerous job about that sawing blade. No place for a fiddler's fingers."

"Does Charlie work close to it?" I had heard about men falling against the screaming saw, losing an arm or even their lives. A chill twisted my shoulders.

"Aye. I say prayers for him every night. Would light a candle for him if I was back in me parish."

"Does he ever speak about me?" I watched a beetle climb a blade of grass. "He didn't ride out that Sunday, like he promised."

"Stiff-necked Englishman! I told him to talk to ye. Not to judge from the gossip."

"But he stayed on."

"Aye, but not a word or a penny from home. Now Charlie's a poor lad like myself."

I felt for the bank check in my pocket. Charlie wouldn't take it if I offered him the money. The horses stomped their legs, and their tails swooshed against Seamus's back.

"That day with Robert," Seamus said softly. "'Twas against your will? You've no interest in that lad?"

"None! I'd kill him if I could!"

"'Twould do no good. Keep your wits, and you'll find a way to teach him a lesson."

"But how can Charlie not understand?"

"Pride. Worrying about buying a farm and his father. You must turn his head." Seamus winked. "Isn't that what you desire?"

"Yes," I said, stunned to realize that's exactly what I wanted. I yearned to see Charlie smile when I teased him, to brush my shoulder against his, or to hear him offer me his handkerchief when I cried. No matter how hard I had tried, I could not weed out these longings.

"But how?" I blushed.

"Talk to Lizzie." One of the horses neighed. "I must go." Seamus squeezed my hand and climbed onto the wagon.

Seamus was right. If any girl understood men, it was my sister.

I found her in a back sitting room with the Yankee gal who clerked at the commissary. Damask curtains tied back with blue satin ribbons allowed sunshine to brighten the dark paneled room. Lizzie and the girl had spread out yards of white lawn on the polished floor, and mounds of lace foamed upon a cherry table. Both of them appeared foolish with their bustled behinds sticking up in the air as they knelt by the sheer fabric.

"Howdy," I said, aware of the dust on my boots, which I'd worn to please my sister. I kicked them off before stepping in by the fabric.

"Good afternoon," Lizzie said, and set down her scissors. Her voice trembled a mite. The Yankee looked at her. "Susanna, please meet my sister, Lavinia." Lizzie's words matched her dress, precise and proper. In the past she'd have said: "This here's my sister, Viney." She couldn't hide her mountain accent, but she had been studying grammar.

"Pleased to meet you." Susanna extended her hand. "Your weaving is beautiful. How I wish I had your talents."

"Thank you." Out of the corner of my eye, I watched Lizzie press her lips together. I supposed it irked her hearing folks always praising her little sister. "What are you sewing?" I asked.

"My trousseau," Lizzie replied. "George sent for the ribbons and lace from France." Her cheeks flushed. "Ordered a huge trunk with our initials carved on it."

I bit back the words: Isn't that an unlucky thing to do *before* the wedding? I stooped and fingered the lawn. "It's lovely, Lizzie. Only machines can spin and weave so fine."

"Yes," Susanna said. "My grandmother worked in the mills at Lowell. A dusty, noisy place."

Lizzie examined my attire. The way I'd sat on the floor had ruffled my skirt and exposed my frayed petticoat.

"If you like, we could cut out new underthings for you. Appears you need them. George ordered several bolts of both lawn and linen." Lizzie's eyes measured my gaze.

"Thank you. I'd like that." I bit my lower lip. "Might even welcome a ruffle on the petticoat."

Now, if Lizzie and I were like those little women in Miss Alcott's book, we would have hugged and kissed, wiping our eyes. But we've never been that sort. I knew we had forgiven each other, but the past had changed our futures. I reckon this was like tying a snapped thread in my warp. There would always be a bump in the coverlet where a knotted thread lay.

While I helped them cut out drawers, petticoats, and camisoles, I studied Susanna. She wore fewer frills than Lizzie, but she was tightly laced, and little jet ear-bobs dangled from her earlobes, sparkling when the sun hit them.

"How's Charlie?" Lizzie finally asked. I could tell by her voice that she had heard about Robert and me.

"Haven't seen him in a spell." I ran a length of edging through my fingers, feeling the lacy flowers united by slender thread. Lizzie and Susanna exchanged glances.

"Mrs. Hill knit that for me," Lizzie said, and took the lace from my hands. "Were you planning to visit Charlie today?"

"No." More looks tossed back and forth between those two. Might as well have been dragonflies the way their eyes darted.

"I reckon . . . I mean . . . I know this is none of my busi-ness, but do you want to see Charlie?" Lizzie asked.

"Yes."

"But—" Lizzie began.

"Blast it all! Why doesn't he come to *me*? Hear my side? Why is he so bullheaded?"

"Maybe you need to turn his head," Susanna said, inspecting a spool of pink ribbons.

"That's what Seamus said."

"Did he?" Lizzie chuckled. "And you are wondering *how* to do that?"

"Yes." I about choked on the word. Felt like a gnat in a spider's web. Lizzie had me trapped, and she knew it.

"Do you know the biblical account of Queen Esther?" Susanna asked. "How she prepared herself to approach her king?"

"Yes. Soaped and scrubbed herself. Dressed grandly. Said all sort of flattery." I didn't like where she was leading. But Charlie had gone caving with her, instead of visiting me. I glanced at her clean fingernails.

"Well?" Lizzie asked. "Do you want our help?"

"Yes," I muttered.

Lizzie stared at me. She probably thought I would never stoop so low. "You'll have to promise to do *everything* we tell you to."

"I'll try."

"Promise. *Everything.* Or I'll not waste my time. I've a wedding to arrange." Lizzie crossed her arms.

"I promise." I wanted to run as soon as I gagged out the words. Lizzie grinned that wicked smile of hers, and Susanna hugged me.

"We'll dress you for the June opening of the library,"

Susanna said. "Everyone will be there. Even Mr. Hughes is coming over for the dedication. And bringing his mother and niece!"

"First we'll cut out those new underthings," Lizzie ordered. "The linen would last the longest. How about this beaded lace for the drawers? With pink ribbons through?"

"And your gown," Susanna crooned as she flipped through a magazine titled *Godey's Lady's Book*.

"Gown? I just sewed two new dresses." I needed the drawers and petticoat, but I had to calm them down a mite.

"The dedication will be a grand occasion. You will need something fine," Susanna said. "Something fetching." She winked at Lizzie.

"How about this?" Lizzie pointed to an illustration of a pert miss in a low-cut dress with a ruffle around the neckline.

"Lizzie! It's not decent!"

"Are you saying that Susanna and I will not be decently attired?"

"No, but . . . you both . . . " I looked down at my chest.

"That's what corsets are for, silly," Susanna said. "And see how a bib can be inserted into the bodice to make it suitable for morning wear? I think, Miss Lavinia, we need to visit the commissary. I'll help you choose the fabric. Let me fetch my bonnet."

"While she does, let me explain how you will make your toilet," Lizzie said.

I folded my hands and made like I was listening to her lecture about brushing my hair a hundred strokes every night, cleaning my fingernails, and scenting my clothes with the lavender sachets she gave me, but instead I wondered if

Charlie ever sat visiting in this room with Susanna. Before she stopped, Lizzie threw in a few more commands about washing my face with milk and rubbing my heels with fine river sand.

"What! Do you think Charlie's going kiss my foot?"

"No, but we'll hope for at least a kiss on your cheek. And you promised to do everything."

I already regretted those words. She would wear them out before all this was finished.

"And come back next Thursday. Su and I have that afternoon off."

I was going to snap off something like "Yes, your highness," but when I looked up, I saw Lizzie's eyes shining with love. She was sharing with me what she knew. So I muttered, "Thank you." And laced up my boots.

Susanna linked arms with me like I was a half-wit and steered me toward the commissary.

"I'm glad that you came today. I've always wanted sisters. I've only brothers at home. You're a year younger than Lizzie, right? I'm so excited that she and George will be moving to Boston. When she's settled, you must come visit." Susanna nodded at a gentleman.

"Boston? I thought they were going to England!" Susanna spoke so rapidly that my brain felt like fleas were biting it.

"Oh, that's right. You weren't talking to each other. Well, George's parents raged against him marrying a servant, but finally his father gave in. He told George that he could take over the family's offices in Boston. Isn't it so romantic, George giving up his London position for Lizzie?"

Poor Lizzie, after all her fine talk about castles and England. But living in Boston meant she could come visit, bringing her babies to the ridge. I felt something inside me relax.

"My papa sent me here for the summer to strengthen me," Susanna chattered on. "He met my mama during the War between the States. She's from Georgia. Papa read how healthy mountain air is. I doubt either of them knew how many boys lived here." She waved at two lads weeding a garden.

"Then, you aren't staying on?" Our boots hit the steps of the commissary. My head ached from Susanna's prattling. Seems she knew the name of every passing gent.

"Oh, no! Papa's sending me to college. Mama says studying is weakening my health, but papa will have his way."

"College! Girls don't do such." Made my brain twirl to think of doing lessons beyond the eighth grade.

"Do so. Lizzie told me how you like to read. I bet you'd be a dandy college student."

One of the lads opened the commissary door, and Susanna smiled at him. Usually it pleasured me to finger the smooth percales and gaze at richly dyed satins, but Susanna chattered as she draped me with chintz and silk. Finally we settled on pink cambric sprinkled with nosegays of blue flowers. Next Susanna heaped hoops, tapes, and boning onto the counter. I closed my eyes while Susanna told the clerk how much of everything to cut.

How much would all this cost, I wondered? I tried to remember the feel of Charlie's fingers against mine.

"Shall I write this on your account, miss?" the clerk asked.

"No." I gave her the bank check and she flipped it over.

"You must endorse it, miss," the clerk said.

I looked at Susanna.

"Silly! You forgot to sign your name." She pointed at the edge.

I grasped the offered pen, dipped it in ink, and wrote out my name. The door opened, and out of the corner of my eye, I noticed Robert enter.

"Shall I credit the remainder to your account?" the clerk asked.

"No, please hand me the cash." I stuffed most of the bills in my pocket but held four dollars in my palm. While Susanna and the clerk babbled and wrapped up a bundle I slipped over to Robert.

"Yes?" He barely looked at me, but went on examining silk cravats. I crunched the heel of my boot on his leather-clad toes.

"Why you . . . " His neck stained red.

I thrust the cash into his hand. "There. We're even. I don't owe you *anything*." I dashed back to Susanna's side.

Chapter Nineteen

Come all ye fair and tender ladies, take a warning
how you court young men . . .
Jean Ritchie, *Singing Family of the Cumberlands*

I only half minded Lizzie's commands. Brushing my hair a hundred strokes tuckered my arm sorely, and I refused to scrub with sand or wash with milk. But I scraped my fingernails clean before I arrived in the sewing room on the next couple of Thursday afternoons. While Lizzie hummed and sewed on her trousseau Susanna helped me stitch my gown. She pinned and basted while I fought down the urge to wiggle.

Near the middle of June, Lizzie set down the napkins she was hemming and circled me. "You'll have to wear this for my wedding," she said. "Only six more weeks and I will be Mrs. George Elsworth." She tugged on my sleeves. "So pretty." She leaned over and kissed my cheek. "My beautiful little sister has grown up."

I'd never seen Lizzie so content. Now that we were talking, it grieved me even more to think of her moving to Boston. Made my throat tighten. Might be years before I would see Lizzie's babies and hear her sing them lullabies. Susanna might speak of me visiting that city, but I couldn't imagine walking on brick streets, hemmed in on both sides by rows of houses. I wouldn't be able to breathe.

"I do pray," Lizzie said, "that the scourge doesn't come early. Spoil my wedding. Though I begged him to wed in June, George wanted to wait until after the opening."

"Scourge?" Susanna muttered through her mouthful of pins.

"Summer fever," I said. "Comes most years in late August. Didn't strike here last year, but a dozen people died over by Jamestown." I turned a few inches as Susanna pulled the pins from her mouth.

"Perhaps the advances in hygiene made by the settlement have banished such diseases," Susanna said. "Hopefully, there's nothing to worry now."

I opened my mouth to protest, but Lizzie pursed her lips and shook her head. How could she tolerate such talk that made the ridge folk sound stupid? Lizzie fussed with the tucked bib inserted into the bodice.

"Charlie will adore you in this frock," Lizzie said, and played a bit more with the neckline. "You'll hold his heart in your hand."

"Who knows," Susanna said as she assisted me out of the underskirt, "you might be a bride yourself before the year's end."

I bent over my sewing. Was that what I was seeking, a wedding? Had I become like the other ridge girls, whose only dream was to marry? Already these afternoons of sewing sucked away at the hours I would have spent weaving. If I had a husband and babies to care for, I would have to weave nights. Such thoughts tumbled in my mind like dust bunnies under a bed. But I missed listening to Charlie chatter about his hoped-for farm and his banter with Seamus. I heard the sawmill when I walked into the settlement and twice Seamus had waved as he drove in a load of logs, but I'd not seen Charlie.

On the morning of the library dedication, I rushed through my chores and served Jacob mush for breakfast.

"Again?" he said. "If'n Charlie don't pay you any mind today, I'll beg him to court you."

"Don't you dare!" I swatted Jacob with a dishrag. "I'll make biscuits and gravy every day for a week starting the morrow."

"Promise? If'n you don't . . . "

"Promise."

After redding up the cabin, I lit out for the settlement. No dew slicked the grass, and the tips of the sassafras shoots drooped. My arms ached from toting water to my garden every day, and I prayed it would rain soon.

Lizzie nodded at me when I stepped into the inn's kitchen. "I'll be up soon. Susanna's waiting for you."

Susanna sat in her drawers, laced and wearing a corset cover with tiny white flowers embroidered on it. She removed the last of her rag curlers and raked her fingers through the ringlets that fringed her face.

"Slip behind there and out of those things." She waved at a two-part wooden screen hung with blue and white toile.

My fingers hurried with my buttons. Part of me was frightened that I'd look like a fool parading in a gown meant for a refined lady, but another part of me wondered what it felt like to float across the lawn in such a full skirt. I pulled on an under petticoat with a deep flounce and stepped into the room.

"Now for the hoops," I said, and eyed the gored petticoat with rows of tape. I'd slipped wire through the tape for stiffening.

"Ah, after I lace you," Susanna said. "Remember how I told you that a corset would enhance your appearance."

"But I didn't wear one when we fitted the gown. I thought—"

"That we'd forgotten? Lizzie knew you'd balk, so after last Thursday, we altered the gown. Without a corset, not one thing will fit. You'll have nothing decent to wear today."

I should have known Lizzie would do something.

"We want what's best for you." Susanna fiddled with her comb.

I sank down on Lizzie's bed and stared at the hundreds of stitches I'd sewn. Yards and yards of gathered frills, even the lily-shaped petticoat had taken hours while dust gathered on my loom. I could have finished those five coverlets in that time.

"Well?" Lizzie asked as she stood in the doorway, grinning.

I folded my arms across my chest and glowered at her.

"You're scared," Lizzie said. "Aren't you? Afraid that you will fail as a charming female."

"No." Never would I admit to my sister that I'd been worrying on that very thought.

"Dare you." Lizzie held up the corset.

"All that work." Susanna shook her curls.

All that time, I wanted to add. I stood up, and they latched onto me.

"Hold the door frame," Lizzie commanded, stuffing me into a linen corset stiff with whalebones. "Suck in your breath."

"You should have been a general . . . " I gasped as she pulled. "Stop it!" I squeaked.

"Still too wide." Lizzie tugged again.

"Don't!" My stomach hit my backbone. The room swirled. I clutched the door frame. Who determined that women should have waists like a wasp?

Lizzie and Susanna shook their heads.

"See, my waist is a whole inch smaller than yours." Susanna leaned against me so I couldn't move.

"And mine is *two* inches smaller." Lizzie stuck a knee in my back and jerked twice. "There. I knotted those laces so they wouldn't give during the day."

"How can I walk if I can't breathe? I might snap in half." I panted, trying to fill my lungs.

"Some nice young gentleman will *have* to assist you," Susanna said as she helped me into the hoops. "After Charlie sees you, you'll wish you had listened to us sooner." She arranged the petticoat while Lizzie buckled the bustle.

"Not too big," I moaned, remembering Lizzie's rear end. I couldn't turn to see how Lizzie had fixed me. I might as well have swallowed a poker I had to stand up so straight.

"Perhaps you will have more respect for us," Lizzie said. "Takes practice to learn how to breathe when laced. To move gracefully in hoops. And remember, Mrs. Hill is always attired properly."

"But Mrs. Hill doesn't prance about in such garb when she weeds her garden."

"Perhaps not," Lizzie asked. "But I've never seen her come to town unlaced and in her everyday dresses."

"Here." Susanna held up a mirror. "I told you laces would heighten your charms."

I glanced at the looking glass and blushed. Appeared the tighter the bony cage was pulled, the more my bosom was pushed up. I wasn't as round as Lizzie, but I had more curves than I had thought possible.

"Cover me up!" I felt the red moving down my neck. Having but a slip of a mirror at home, I'd never seen so much of my body exposed. I stepped into the underskirt.

"Certainly." Lizzie guided my arms into the bodice and buttoned me up as Susanna arranged the ruffled underskirt.

"Where's the bib?" I looked down at my exposed front. Only a little ruffle edged the neckline where I had inserted a lacy fabric. "You changed this!"

"Did we?" Lizzie laughed and patted my cheek. "But we added that delightful frill." She unbuttoned her dress. "Su will fix your hair while I change. Mrs. Hill said to look for her. I can't wait to see Charlie's face."

If I could have bent, I would have walloped Lizzie, but all I could do was sit and feel the sweat dripping down between my shoulder blades. Susanna fussed and combed until I thought she'd pull every hair from my head. Finally, she slipped me a pair of white lace gloves.

"Every lady covers her hands. I bought them just for you."

My hands, calloused and firm, didn't belong in lacy gloves. But I didn't want to hurt Susanna's feelings. I tugged them on, trying to fit my fingers into the slim tubes. All the fight left me as my hands disappeared. I wanted to weep. Like a little lapdog, I followed Lizzie and Susanna to the veranda, where George greeted us pleasantly before linking his arm with Lizzie's. Susanna opened her parasol, and together we minced across the gravel path toward the library.

My eyes searched the crowd gathered in front of the gray, squatty library with a tin roof. Mr. Hughes's red hair shone amidst the bobbing waves of straw hats and ladies' flower-covered bonnets. Susanna and I steered our skirts through the chattering clusters of men and women. Finally, I spied Charlie and Seamus standing near Mr. and Mrs. Hill. My palms sweated in the tight gloves. Had Charlie noticed me? I liked the blue-striped shirt he wore with his rose-colored waistcoat.

"Susanna!" A girl in a frilly green silk approached us, and I recognized her as one of the trio who had criticized my clothing at the New Year's Eve party.

"Good morning, Victoria," Susanna said. "Please meet Lizzie's sister, Viney."

"Pleased to meet you." I stuck out my gloved hand, hoping she couldn't feel my damp palms through her gloves.

"What an adorable frock," Victoria crooned. "Such a cunning bodice. I wish had one like it. Promise me that you and Susanna will come for tea this week so that we can become better acquainted."

"Thank you." I bobbed my head, wondering what Miss Victoria would think if I arrived in homespun and barefoot. Were all the English this fickle? But for some odd reason, her words strengthened me, made me lift my chin. Acting like a lady wasn't that hard.

"We'll schedule tea soon," Susanna said, and guided me toward the Hills.

"Good morning, ladies," Mr. Hill said. "Two of the fairest flowers in our midst."

"You are lovely." Mrs. Hill kissed our cheeks and wrapped an arm around my waist. "So sweet. Don't you think so, lads?"

"Thank you, ma'am." I glanced at Charlie, but he would not meet my gaze.

"Beautiful," Seamus said, and nudged Charlie.

"Yes, lovely," Charlie mumbled.

"I shall leave Viney in your care, gentlemen," Susanna said, "as I promised John Mason that I would attend the dedication with him." She squeezed my hand and floated away.

"Here you are!" Mr. Hughes strode up, accompanied by an older woman wearing a black frock and a younger lady in a dainty lawn dress and straw bonnet.

"Mother, Emily, I would like you to meet a talented weaver. A mountain artist." Mr. Hughes's eyes swept over me. "And a charming young lady."

We shook hands. But I felt queer having these men tell me I was beautiful, and nary a smile from Charlie. What ailed him? Had he set his heart against me?

"I hope we can be friends," Emily said. "I am learning to make photographs and would like to take some of your work. Uncle Thomas showed me your weavings used in the Tabard."

"Come visit anytime," I replied, and noticed the smile Miss Emily gave Seamus.

"Ladies," Mr. Hill said, "we should move closer. The dedication will begin momentarily. Shall we?" He gave his arm to Mrs. Hughes.

Seamus escorted Miss Emily, and Charlie nodded at me. My fingers gripped his forearm and my skirt swished against his trousers as we stepped through the double doorway and into the library.

I inhaled the scent of leather. Bound in red, blue, and green, and stamped with gold lettering, books filled the shelves that lined the room. Never had I seen so many books. I thought of our worn Bible and Webster's *Blue Back Speller* at home. But Charlie's eyes showed no surprise, as I reckon that his family owned heaps of books. We glided over to a corner away from the long walnut tables surrounded by polished chairs. A woman could unfold three yards of calico across those tables.

Everyone hushed when Mr. Hughes began to speak. I only half listened as he jawed on about the great literary and educational opportunities abounding between the library's walls. I inched closer to the back row, where I had spied two books I itched to open: *The Lives of Celebrated Female Sovereigns* and *Six Life Studies of Famous Women*. Except for Betsy Ross and Martha Washington, I'd never studied on women. I nipped one from the shelf and began to read.

Mr. Hughes finished his speech, folks clapped and

drifted about. Suddenly, I smelled bay rum, and looked up at Robert and two other tall gentlemen. I felt their stares inch over me and linger on the rise and fall of my bosom. In the press of people, I couldn't escape. I hated everything I wore, from the boned bodice that stuck to me like a second skin to the stiff petticoats that hindered walking.

"How fetching." Robert gripped my hand and kissed it. "May I assume you have come to your senses? Discovered your female charms? Perhaps we should renew our friendship."

I fought the corset for air. I couldn't spy Charlie, but what would he think if he saw me with Robert?

"You should share, Robert," one of the lads said. "Aren't you going to introduce us to this winsome lass?"

I thought about heaving the book at Robert, but didn't want to harm it. Robert would ruin *everything*. I had to do something. How *did* Lizzie handle men?

"Please to meet you," I stammered. "Isn't it a bit stuffy in here?"

"Right," Robert said. "Allow me the pleasure of escorting you to the Tabard's veranda. To take some refreshments, together."

That was the *last* thing I wanted. Tears prickled my eyelids. At that moment, as the two gents backed away, a familiar skirt rustled near us.

"Gentlemen," Lizzie cooed. "I see that you have discovered my sweet sister." She slipped an arm around my waist. "Please forgive me, but I must snatch her from your midst." She took the book from my hands and placed it on the shelf. "Silly goose, reading! We mustn't keep Charlie and George waiting."

Lizzie ushered me around the tall bookshelves. Tears wet my cheeks. I muffled my sobs with my hands. Why had I thought I could be a flirt?

"Shh, all's well." Lizzie patted my shoulder, and we paused between the shelves.

"How," I asked, "did you know?"

"I suspected trouble when I saw those three huddled about someone, short, then I recognized your skirt."

"Thank you." My breath came in short gasps. "I'm no good at all this. And you're so . . . so in control." I might not agree with all her ways, but Lizzie didn't blunder like me.

"Shush now. A lady should focus her attention on her gentleman. Charlie *is* waiting."

Charlie's grim face had softened. Lizzie placed my hand on his arm.

"She's so rattled. I believe you're the only one who can stop those tears. And she needs fresh air."

He guided me to one side of the library, away from the exiting crowd and into the shade of two oak trees. I wept, all stiff like a wooden doll, until Charlie leaned my head against his shoulder. I rested my cheek next to his satin waistcoat and inhaled lavender. He pulled a freshly ironed handkerchief from his breast pocket.

"It's clean."

"Thank you. Oh, Charlie, why didn't you come that Sunday?" I snuffled into the linen.

"I was angry. Didn't know who to believe." Charlie rolled his hat brim between his fingers and started to pace.

"But how could you believe Robert? You know I detest him. How could you doubt me?"

"I kept hoping I'd see you when you came to town, but you never walked by the mill. Always stayed at the inn, where Robert lives."

Seems I had tangled up everything once again. "But I only wanted to avoid seeing that saw. Hearing it slice trees."

"And today when I saw your fine attire, I figured you were following Lizzie's lead, hoping to marry up."

"I'm not like her!" But hadn't I tried to act like her today? "You escorted me to the opening. Why?"

"Because the Hills asked me to."

"And now?" My heart felt limp.

"I watched your face when Robert approached you. Part scared. Part angry. You showed no interest in those fellows. And your tears showed me the truth."

God bless Lizzie. I vowed to never look down on her again or take her for granted.

Charlie took my hands in his. "Please, one more question." His eyes examined me from my dusty boots to his green ribbon in my hair. "Is this what you truly want?" he asked.

"No."

"Then, why?"

"For you. To catch your eye."

"And every lad on the ridge!" He glanced at my low neckline. I felt the red swoop up my neck and to my cheeks.

"Wasn't supposed to be so low. Lizzie and Susanna altered it. Dared me." My voice began to quiver.

"I should have known." Charlie leaned back against the tree and gazed at me. "You are beautiful, lovelier than any other girl here, but you aren't the woman I admire. I prefer you in homespun with dirt under your fingernails. That is the Viney

I've missed." He looked over at the Tabard. "They've begun serving."

Let them, I thought. My stomach was too compressed to eat. And I didn't want to share Charlie with anyone.

"We should join them. Unless you'd rather walk to where we can talk and be alone? Perhaps to the lookout?"

I wanted to take Charlie's hand and run through the woods, but I would never find the breath to race to the overlook. If only I hadn't given in to Lizzie and Susanna and had kept on my everyday clothes. My clothes!

"If'n you'll wait outside the kitchen, I could pack us a bite to eat."

"Certainly." Charlie smiled and offered me his arm.

We slipped around to the kitchen. I shoved open the door and smelled baked ham and yeast rolls. Janie stared at me and giggled.

"Don't you dare laugh! Help! Get me out of this, please." I wobbled up the back stairs in the hoops, pulling off the dratted gloves. Standing in Lizzie's room, I escaped from the bodice and stepped out of the hoops. Janie jerked on the laces, the knot gave, and I collapsed on Lizzie's bed.

"You're crushing your gown!" Janie pulled the dress from under me.

"Don't care. The only bones I plan to wear from now on are my own ribs." I threw the gloves at the ceiling.

Janie smoothed the skirt and carefully hung up the overdress while I slipped into my blue calico.

"All those yards and yards of cloth," Janie said. "Lizzie did you up fine."

"Too grand. I'll never wear that again." I watched Janie caress the ruffled skirt. She sighed as she pulled her hands from the soft fabric. She was taller than me, a mite thinner. And she'd rescued me from more scrapes than I wanted to think about.

"Why don't you take it? Wear it for Sam." I kicked my boots beneath Lizzie's bed and wiggled my toes. "Let out the seams and you won't need a corset."

Janie's mouth gaped. "You're joshing?"

"Nope. I never want to be seen in that dress. And if you want a bit more to cover your front, ask Lizzie to sew in the bib for the bodice. Won't Sam be tickled to see you so refined?"

"For our wedding!" Janie flung herself at me. "I've dreamed of something beautiful to wear, but never as lovely as this." She kissed my cheek. "Thank you. Thank you!"

"It's all yours. Now, could I have some of those rolls and little cakes I saw in the kitchen?" I pulled myself from her embrace. "And how about a bottle of lemonade? Charlie's waiting." I loved saying those words and hurried after Janie to the kitchen, where we packed a basket. Charlie opened the back door, and we made toward Wilson's lookout.

"Should have left your boots home," I teased Charlie. "Nothing better than feeling the dirt between my toes." Feathery hemlock branches brushed my shoulders, and a squirrel scolded us as we headed down the trail. A few late rosy blossoms floated in a sea of dusty green rhododendron leaves. Charlie had removed his cravat and waistcoat and rolled up his sleeves.

"We dearly need a rain." Charlie swung the basket back and forth.

"But not today." I danced backward up the path, watching the muscles in Charlie's forearms tighten and release. "Tonight, maybe."

"Probably not. My barometer hasn't fallen."

We skirted a couple of large sandstone boulders and stepped into a narrow clearing. Wrinkles flowed off the ridge like rumpled calico. I loved the mottled swirls of green where hemlock, beech, and oak mingled. I glanced at Charlie, but he was gazing skyward.

"So beautiful. I love this spot. The only place where I can see an expanse of sky."

I shielded my eyes from the sun. A haze lay over the eastern mountains. A buzzard drifted overhead. Charlie's hand slid down my arm and twined with my fingers. As rough as his hand was, he must be working the logs without gloves.

"Later, after the sun warms the air even more, clouds might form," Charlie said. "Must be past noon. Shall we have our picnic in the shade? Beastly hot."

Charlie spread the blanket beneath a chestnut, and we sank down on the cushion of grass. Wind tickled the blooming daisies that surrounded us. I lifted out napkins heavy with cress sandwiches, buttered rolls filled with ham, and tiny chocolate cakes. Janie had packed china plates, and glasses for the lemonade.

It pleasured me to watch Charlie eat. I nibbled a roll, but my innards were still rearranging themselves. While Charlie consumed the picnic, he chattered about how he hated the whine of the saw blade and the sawdust that reddened his eyes. He told how his friend Harry had almost lost a hand; after that, Charlie had taken a job stacking boards. Charlie explained how after the mill closed, he and Seamus hoed in the settlement's tomato fields until dark. Weariness smudged darkness beneath his eyes, and he'd thinned down, too.

"Such a feast!" Charlie leaned back. "And thank God for a day of rest."

"Is that how you've been spending the Sabbath? Resting?" I asked as I collected the linens and china and fitted them into the basket.

"Hmmm, yes." Charlie sighed and reached for my hand. His breathing deepened.

I leaned on one elbow and watched Charlie nap. I knew Charlie was tuckered from those long days, as cockcrow came early in June, but I had hoped we would talk more. And I was certain that Lizzie's fellars hadn't fallen asleep when they courted her. She kept them laughing. Even Hazel made Jacob chatter. Was I so dull? Reckoned I needed to ask Lizzie for more advice. A beetle raced across the blanket toward us, and I flipped him away. Loosening my fingers from Charlie's grasp, I eased back on the blanket and dozed.

I awoke to air moving as Charlie shooed a deerfly away from my face with his hat. Through half-closed eyes I drank in the look on Charlie's face. I'd seen the same expression on George that day at the spring. Charlie wanted to kiss me. The memory of Robert's touch shot through me, and my breathing quickened. But kissing Charlie would be my choice. His fingers brushed the deerfly from my hair.

"Biting flies mean rain," I said, and wondered how those

words had come out. The shadows had lengthened while we napped.

Charlie rose. "Should be heading back. I'll borrow a horse and ride you home."

I watched Charlie's shoulders as he stretched. What would it feel like to be held in those arms? After folding the blanket, he took my hand, and we strolled toward the settlement listening to the chipping of a cardinal. I paused and plucked a daisy from a low clump and stuck it in his top buttonhole.

"A flower to remember today by." Kiss me, I wanted to add, feeling a warmth I'd never known. But Charlie only smiled.

We ducked the last hemlock branches before hitting the road and quickened our pace when we saw the doctor's buggy roll up to the inn. All the windows in the Tabard were lit. The doctor jumped from his carriage, and Seamus took hold of the halter.

"Someone hurt?" Charlie called.

"George and two other lads collapsed with high fevers."

"The summer scourge," I whispered. But it had come too soon. 'Twas merely late June, not August.

Lizzie burst from the kitchen. "Viney! Where have you been? George's bad off." She flung her arms about me.

"The doctor's come. He'll know what to do," Charlie said.

"George can't die." Lizzie's tears wet my shoulder. "He never should have had those initials carved on our trunk. Bad luck, for certain."

Chapter Twenty

*The unfortunate appearance of typhoid fever in our
midst . . . has rendered the publication of*
The Rugbeian *impossible.*

The Rugbeian

*A*s soon as I finished my chores, I lit out for the settlement. I had to find out if Charlie and Lizzie were safe. Not a cloud shadowed the sun, and my toes sunk into soft, dry dust. If it didn't rain soon, the corn would be puny. The heat thickened the air, and my bodice clung to my back.

Felt queer not to hear the sawmill when my feet hit the main road. The rising temperature had silenced the birds, but horses neighed at the inn. I rounded a curve and saw a half-dozen wagons circled at the Tabard. Many of my neighbors' mules and hired teams from Sedgemore lined the streets in front of boardinghouses and homes. Men toted trunks and carpetbags. Women hastened behind them with baskets, clinging to children. All the hooves and wheels had churned up a fine haze of dust that gritted my lips. Outside the Tabard, Charlie and Seamus heaved trunks onto a wagon bed, but turned before I could wave. At least those two lads were still healthy.

I skirted around to the back and pushed open the kitchen door. Heaps of dirty dishes surrounded Lizzie, and baskets of soiled laundry spilled out of the washroom and into the kitchen. Lizzie's curls flew every which way, and the imprint of where she'd dried her hands stained her apron.

"Oh, Viney, I hoped you'd come." Lizzie's eyes were red from weeping. "Everyone's leaving."

"Where's Janie?"

"Sam came for her. Said he'd marry her today if need be to keep her away from the typhoid. I can't leave George!"

"Mrs. Johnstone?" While talking, Lizzie had washed the same cup five times.

"Packing. Doctor took George to a boardinghouse turned into a hospital. Need to separate the ones with typhoid fever. Doctor said it's deadly."

"So that's their name for the fever, typhoid?" I shoved her away. "Here. Let me finish. Did you sleep a'tall?"

Lizzie shook her head. "Stayed with George till they moved him. Doctor won't let me into the men's ward. Not fitting."

"You go rest. Have a little nap." I pushed Lizzie toward the stairs.

Between the heat from the cookstove and the blasted sun, I about died washing that mound of dishes. Although typhoid was serious, didn't these foreigners have any grit? Who was going to nurse these folks? I sloshed water and thumped down the cast-iron pots. Finally, I walked out onto the front veranda to catch the breeze and to see if anyone would be needing a noon meal. Mr. Hughes and Mr. Hill talked beside a small oak. Only two wagons remained, and they were preparing to ride out. Seamus sat on the seat of one of the wagons, but when Charlie saw me, he jumped off of his wagon.

"You shouldn't be here." He trotted up to the porch.

"I'm no coward," I snapped.

"Please, go home." Charlie took my hand. "You're not safe here. The doctor thinks the Tabard's well is to blame. The water was contaminated by typhoid bacteria that formed from meat cooling in the well."

So this wasn't the summer scourge, but a plague of the foreigners' own making, not that it mattered now.

"And what about you and Seamus?"

"We're camped out in a tent, hauling water from the stream." Charlie lifted his hat and fanned his face. He needed a shave, and the sun washed all the color from his face. But his eyes shone with the deep blue of the sunset when the last light slips away.

"Charlie!" Seamus called.

"Go home, please." Charlie brushed my cheek with his fingers and ran for his wagon.

"Who do you think you are, telling me what to do?" I muttered as Charlie's back faded in a swirl of dust. But I felt the tips of his fingers on my cheek and cherished the concern in his voice.

Lizzie stumbled into the kitchen that afternoon. Between the two of us, we hauled water from the stable's well, boiled the laundry, and wrestled with sheets until my arms felt like wet yarn. A heap of linen still waited in the washroom, but I shook my head.

"Can't do it all in one day, even when sunset comes late! No one's staying here. Charlie says the well's gone bad."

"I can't live here all alone!" Lizzie's eyes clutched mine.

"Where's Susanna?" How was I going to attend to all my chores if Lizzie wouldn't let me go home? Who'd water our garden?

"Ill. Mrs. Hill took her to the ladies' ward."

"Why don't we go see how she's faring?"

The only traffic was the few stragglers stacking luggage near hitching posts. Doors banged. Feet tramped down wooden steps. A dog barked. Lizzie led me to a mustard-colored board-and-batten house. The air smelled of baked wood and hot dust.

"They bedded George upstairs." Lizzie's eyes scanned the upper story windows.

We slipped in, letting out a fly that bounced against the screen door. In the parlor Mrs. Hill and the doctor spoke quietly. Mrs. Hill beckoned for us to enter.

"George?" Lizzie asked.

"She's his betrothed," Mrs. Hill told the doctor.

"His fever is still rising." The doctor paused. "A very ill lad. Serious dysentery. You must not visit him."

I could tell Lizzie wouldn't heed the warning by the way George's locket bobbed on her chest and her eyes hardened. Another bullheaded Walker, she was as stubborn as a sow at a feeding trough and would do her best to climb those stairs.

"How's Susanna, sir?" I asked.

"We don't think she has typhoid," the doctor said. "She's resting comfortably."

"Viney." Mrs. Hill pulled me aside. "Could you stay on at the inn? Help out for a few days?"

"Well . . . I haven't finished all the coverlets Mr. Foster ordered."

"There's no need to hurry with the coverlets. Few visitors will come until they know Rugby is safe again."

"Yes, ma'am."

"For the time being, why don't you and Lizzie move into the rooms just above the kitchen. It'll be cooler on the second story."

"Yes, ma'am."

For the rest of that week, I spooned water between Susanna's lips and helped Lizzie cook for the few lads that stayed. We hauled water from the stable's well and washed the mounds of soiled linens that I carried from the sick ward. Seemed queer to sleep in a feather bed in a pine-paneled room with a polished wood floor. I would awake to the first rays of dawn glowing through curtains that covered tall windows. Before I fell asleep at night, I'd stare out at the dark settlement houses that put me in mind of giant stumps left to rot along the dusty road.

I relished the meal times when Charlie and Seamus pulled a chair to the great mahogany table in the Tabard. My shoulder brushed Charlie's as I set down bowls of new potatoes and peas. Seamus winked at us.

Most nights, Charlie and Seamus labored in the tomato fields until they couldn't see the flash of their hoes, and then fell into bed. But after twilight on Thursday, they stumbled onto the veranda. Charlie and I sank down on the stoop, and he leaned his head on my shoulder. Seamus opened his new fiddle case.

"Music," Seamus said. "We need music."

He began with slow airs that curled inside us, squeezing our souls, seeping into our weariness. I wanted to weep, but was too tired to find tears. Seamus slid into a hornpipe, then quickened us with a reel. If his fingers had been flint, we'd have seen sparks. Finally, he nudged Charlie with his toe and began a waltz.

Charlie pulled me to my feet. With both hands on each other's shoulders, we glided around the veranda. I licked my lips, hoping Charlie would kiss me, but when the tune ended, he just hugged me.

"Thank you. Take care, Viney, please."

"And you, too. Sleep well."

Despite the heat I climbed to the top of the Tabard, to that little room that looked like an eye watching the settlement. I scanned the woods for the glow of a lantern, trying to locate the lads' tent. Like a patch of foxfire, I saw the yellow flicker and fade just west of the inn.

"Good night," I whispered above the hum of the tree frogs.

Friday afternoon Charlie opened the kitchen door. "Lizzie?"

Lizzie threw down the green onions she was chopping and ran. I dashed to the veranda with Charlie following. Heat waves blurred the red calico racing down the road, skirts lifted high enough to show a flash of black stocking.

"George?" I asked, and took Charlie's hand.

"Breathing his last." Charlie leaned against the post,

clenching and unclenching his jaw, squeezing my hand until my fingers turned white.

"I met George in the first form at the school Rugby's named after. He gave me the answers for Latin, and I helped him in natural science. Lizzie changed him. He went from being a selfish boy to a man ready to marry, to sacrifice for his wife. He was happy."

"Lizzie was, too. Content."

We walked hand in hand down the deserted street. Little puffs of dust rose from our footfalls. Sweat flowed down my breastbone. Cracks crazed the dirt, and grass had browned. Susanna looked up from a rocker on the boardinghouse porch. Tears streaked her cheeks.

"Upstairs. Second room on the right."

I took the steps two at a time, heading toward Lizzie, who rocked back and forth. She knelt next to a cot, holding George's hand, which was slick with her tears. Mrs. Hill was trying to cover him, and her face relaxed when she saw me. I dropped down beside my sister.

"Lizzie, Lizzie," I crooned. "Be letting go now. It's over. I'll take you home."

"Never." She shook her head.

I wrapped my arms about her and could feel her shoulder blades. She had eaten so little lately, and had even left off her laces. Lizzie dug her face into George's side and sobbed as I pried her shaking body away.

"They'll put him in a box! A box!"

"Shh." I rubbed the Lizzie's back. My tears darkened her red calico. "Come away, please. There's naught more you can do."

"Our wedding! Only ten more days."

"I know. I know."

Lizzie lifted her crumbled face. "You don't *know*. You can't understand." She choked on her words. "I'd have done anything for George. Anything! Even stay *here*!"

Charlie helped me pull Lizzie away, and together, we helped her down the stairs, and she collapsed onto a love seat.

"Here, dear." Mrs. Hill tipped a cup to Lizzie's lips. "Drink this."

Lizzie tried to push her away, but between sobs she sucked in some of the liquid.

"I gave her laudanum," Mrs. Hill said. "Take her to the inn. Put her to bed."

Charlie and I escorted Lizzie back up the street and into her room. After Charlie trudged away, I slipped Lizzie out of her frock and into a nightgown. She curled into a tiny ball and fell asleep.

Monday early while pumping water, I watched Charlie and Seamus dig George's grave in the new cemetery. Their pickax and shovel rang against the baked earth. I knew Charlie wiped more than sweat from his eyes as he dragged his sleeve across his face.

Back in the Tabard's kitchen, I set down my buckets, and the thunk echoed through the hallway. Silence filled the inn, and the entire settlement. The foreigners I had longed to be shut of had run away. Now George wouldn't take my sister from me. I had what I had longed for, but felt no satisfaction.

* * *

Susanna and I linked arms around Lizzie, who was dressed in black, with only the silver locket, glinting like the moon, upon her bodice. We followed George's coffin, carried by Charlie, Seamus, Mr. Hill, and Mr. Hughes. Mrs. Hill came next with the few remaining settlers, plus Jacob and Hazel. Ten days ago, I had minced down this path in a corset and bustle. Now I wore one of Lizzie's old work dresses dyed black.

George's funeral was a quiet affair, unlike the hollering heard during a mountain burial. The preacher, like a giant white moth, raised his arms and quoted the Good Book. Mr. Hughes praised George's noble spirit. Lizzie stared at the men, shaking. Sweat trickled down everyone's faces, but my sister quivered from the frost settling into her heart. I kept thinking she would wail, as such were our ways. When Charlie and Seamus threw the first shovels full of dirt onto the coffin, Lizzie broke free and jumped into the hole.

"Bury me, too!" she screamed, and tossed dirt over her. "Bury me, too!"

"Lizzie!" I scrambled down the rough clay walls. Lizzie beat on me, but I grabbed her wrists. Dust stung my nose. Pebbles fell, and Jacob stood near me. He scooped up Lizzie.

"Here." Charlie knelt, hands extended. He lifted Lizzie out of the grave. She fell into a heap.

Mrs. Hill and Susanna took Lizzie back to the Tabard, but I waited for Charlie. Even after the men had filled the hole and the others had drifted away, Charlie stood staring at the mound of dirt. Shoulders bent, face streaked with dust, and his fingers gray with grime, he leaned on his shovel.

"Come," I said, and took his hand.

187

"Where?" He glanced at me, and I longed to wash the sorrow from his eyes.

"To the river. Cooler there."

Charlie trudged beside me down the twisted path to the Clear Fork. Ferns had faded yellow, and grass lay flat on the hard clay. The air beneath the canopy of leaves trapped the afternoon heat and wrapped it around us. When we reached the river, Charlie dropped onto the rock where that hoppytoad lived.

Dipping my apron in the water, I wiped his face. Charlie closed his eyes and sighed, allowing the icy water to run down his neck and onto that golden hair I yearned to touch. I washed his hands and cooled a blister rising on his palm. We rested on the rocks, listening to the river trickle over the pebbles and flow around the ridge. I dangled my toes in the current, feeling the water wash away some of my grief.

I yearned to wrap my arms about Charlie, to give him the strength I drew from my mountain. But what would that act mean for both of us? Finally, I buried my face in the folds of his linen shirt, flax spun by English fingers. How I wish my own fingers had created that shirt that rested on his skin. Charlie drew his arms around me; his hands rested on my waist.

"Thank you, Viney." He kissed my cheek. "I love your grit. I love you."

I had never dreamed I would long to hear those words from a man, especially a foreigner. My lips answered. I took Charlie's face in my hands and kissed him. He inhaled. My own breathing quickened when his mouth sought mine. I felt like a fluff of wool ready to be spun by Charlie's hands. Now I understood the yearning that had swept over Lizzie that day at the spring.

"Viney, Viney." Charlie cupped my face in his calloused hands. "We must go back."

Our eyes met, and I knew we were battling the same longings. He stood and pulled me to my feet, yet his hands remained around my waist.

"I love your scent, of strong soap, wool, and something sweet." His lips brushed mine. "Come."

We climbed slowly up the trail, arms around each other. I remembered seeing Jacob and Hazel in the spring woods, and knew they must have felt the same giddiness. Twilight sifted over us, and the first fireflies flashed their lanterns. With one last, long kiss before he opened the inn's door, Charlie bid me good night.

I tiptoed into Lizzie's room and found her sitting by her trunk, sobbing into a mound of camisoles and petticoats.

"Oh, Lizzie." I knelt beside her and reached for the crumbled garments, but she clutched them closer. "I'm so sorry. Truly I am. I wish there was something I could do."

"I dreamed of coming to George in the finest lawn, with ribbons and laces. Pure. Chaste. One week and I'd have been his wife."

I felt the press of Charlie's lips on mine and how my skin still tingled on my cheeks where he'd touched me. I realized that no words could comfort Lizzie. I squirmed in the knowing and the heat rising in me.

Lizzie lifted her face and stared at me in the thread of moonlight. She scanned my rumpled clothing and fly-away hair.

"You've been with Charlie."

"Yes." I looked out the window at the constellation of fireflies.

"He kissed you, didn't he?"

I heard the grief in her voice. Lizzie scooted closer, into the silver light. Her hair rippled across her nightgown. There would be plenty of fellars longing to take George's place, but would my sister want them?

"Didn't he?" she repeated, and took my hands.

"Well, in truth, I kissed him *first*. But only after he told me that he loved me." I felt Lizzie's eyes absorbing me as I leaned against the wooden frame of the bed. I felt shy confessing such on the day she had buried her beloved.

"Your first kiss. And you're hungering for more. Aren't you?"

"Yes." I wondered what Lizzie would think if I told how we had stopped on the path and kissed until I was dizzy? She touched my cheek.

"Take care with kissing, Viney." Tears glittered in her eyes.

"I will." I inhaled her rose perfume. Lizzie was right. Like some wild yeast, I could feel the wanting expanding, bubbling up inside me.

"Here." Lizzie dropped the underthings on my lap. "Save them for *your* wedding night." Tears slipped across her cheeks again.

"Lizzie . . . time to go to sleep." I had to move her mind away from all of this.

"I couldn't sleep. My thoughts plague me." She twisted her curls in her fingers. "Please, stay with me. It'd comfort me to have you close, like when we were girls."

"I'll stay with you."

Chapter Twenty-one

*Accounts of the extreme heat of the present Summer
season are pouring in from all quarters of
the globe, certainly Rugby is of no exception.*
The Rugbeian

Over the next few weeks the settlement buried three more boys. Charlie and Seamus dug the graves and hauled rocks for the headstones. Finally, the last patient walked out of the temporary hospital and the doctor declared Rugby free of typhoid. A couple of guests even straggled in, escaping the heat of Knoxville. Mr. Hughes had left for England, but had stopped in Boston and hired on a Mr. Walton to manage the Tabard. The week after the Walton family arrived, I spoke with Lizzie.

"I can't stay on. I need to be weaving, seeing to the garden."

"Don't leave me. Please." Lizzie snatched my hand. "I keep waking in the middle of the night. Feeling you nearby quiets me."

Lizzie had dyed all her dresses black and even tucked George's silver locket inside her bodice. Some days she forgot to eat until I fixed her a plate and watched her nibble it.

"Folks are returning to their houses. Saw more lighted windows last night. Mr. Walton will hire another cook. Or you could come along with me, move home."

"I can't be so far from George." Lizzie turned her eyes on me. "Please stay."

Every evening she sat by George's grave, whispering, weeping. No wonder she couldn't sleep, after those hours in a graveyard. Perhaps I should stay awhile longer.

"I'll think on it." I hugged Lizzie and marched toward home.

I had slipped back to the cabin now and then to throw my shuttle. At first, I thought it odd that I had found the garden hoed and watered, the cabin free of dust. Finally, Jacob had muttered something about Hazel tidying up the place, but wouldn't look me in the eye.

My toes sank into the dust coating the trail leading home. The woods were tinder dry and silent. Wells would run out if rain didn't come soon. I ducked below the service-berry bush at the edge of the trail and walked into our clearing. Voices tumbled from the porch. Climbing the steps, I found Hazel setting on Jacob's lap, buttoning her bodice.

"When's the wedding?" I asked, feeling my own cheeks flush.

"Last week." Jacob grinned. "Still celebrating." He kissed Hazel.

"Last week! But you didn't tell us! Why weren't Lizzie and I invited?"

"Didn't seem fit," Hazel said. "What with Lizzie grieving. And with you nursing, being near the fever and all . . . "

"Seemed best to wed quietlike," Jacob interrupted. "Past

month Hazel's been caring for the garden, washing, cooking supper for me."

I sank onto one of the splint-bottom chairs and stared at Jacob's hand on Hazel's waist. I had thought that by the time these two wed, Charlie would have bought land. I couldn't stay here and listen to their cornshuck mattress rustle at night.

"You can still live with us," Hazel said. "I'm proud to have you as my new sister."

"Thank you. I'm right happy for you and Jacob. You're the perfect wife for him." And she was. Hazel was hardworking, sweet tempered, and never sassed her pa. She was a year younger than me and adored Jacob. After years of quarreling with Lizzie and me, I reckoned my brother felt like the top dog in a pack of hounds.

"I'll need to finish that warp before I can move my loom," I replied. "Lizzie's wanting me to spend nights with her. She can't sleep without me nearby." I didn't tell Jacob and Hazel about how most nights I found Lizzie by her trunk, weeping into her sheets and pillows. Jacob looked relieved.

"Sounds fittin'. Weave here days, spend nights at the settlement. How's Charlie?" Jacob asked.

"Dog tired. Hoeing tomatoes and hauling water. Only a few lads have returned since the quarantine was lifted." What Jacob wanted to know was if Charlie was courting me, but I wasn't telling.

"We'd have lost the garden if'n Hazel hadn't toted water. Been a real blessing." Jacob's hand squeezed Hazel's waist. She snuggled closer and smiled at him like he was a tom turkey strutting and fanning his tail. "Time we get back to hoeing."

"Could you mind the fire?" Hazel asked. "So I can hoe? I'll be in later to drop the dumplings."

"Surely." I pulled open the screen door and stomped to my loom. With the look in Jacob's eyes, doubt if they hoed many rows before noon. Queer how watching Hazel and Jacob stroll away arm in arm made my insides quiver. I wondered what it would feel like to sit on Charlie's lap and rest my head on his shoulder. Most nights Charlie and Seamus stopped by the inn, but Charlie vowed we were never to be alone again.

"In my country," he had said, "courting couples are chaperoned. Such customs . . . ah . . . prevent indiscretions."

I wanted to say, But didn't you leave your country because you were weary of all those rules? Mountain men guarded their daughters, but they allowed courting couples moments in the shadow of a porch corner or the overhanging branches of a pine. Lizzie and George had never paid any mind to such rules. But that stiff-necked Charlie had set his jaw. Sunday evenings Seamus would fiddle while Charlie sat next to me on the back porch steps, holding my hand. Now and then his arm would creep around my waist. Mostly he talked about his plans for his farm. I could tell by the way Charlie would sometimes look away that he was fighting the same battle that rose inside me.

I picked up my shuttle and brushed off the dust. My feet danced across the treadles. With my right hand I threw the shuttle, and with my left I whacked the beater. As soon as I finished this warp, I'd move the loom. The pattern grew, and I turned six more inches onto the breast beam. But where could I live? I could spend nights with Lizzie, but I couldn't bring my loom and wheel to the Tabard. If only Charlie would hurry and buy his land. Should I make mention to him that I needed a home? Thinking about Charlie slowed my hands. I drifted into a sweetness where I could feel his lips on mine and his breath in my ear. I floated away and heard the gurgle of the river rushing over the rocks. But now and then, my head bobbed above the current, and I pondered this part of me that had fruited. A year ago, even a few months past, I hadn't realized how love made a body tender. It was as if a set of cards had combed bits of chaff from me— mulish thoughts about men, misguided ideas about Lizzie and George. Those cards kept pulling me back and forth, rearranging my mind until my heart was a soft cloud of fleece that Charlie spun into a thread of love. Now I envied Jacob and Hazel instead of thinking them foolish. The screen door snapped shut.

"Been busy?" Hazel asked, and hung her sunbonnet on Lizzie's old peg. "Can you stay for dinner?" She reached for the flour and eggs.

"Yes, thank you. What day did y'all wed?"

"Last Sunday evening. My mama told Jacob that it wasn't proper for me to keep coming here, since you weren't at home. My daddy said he'd have no shotgun weddings in our family, so best to hitch up while the preacher was here."

"So after Sunday meeting, the preacher person came to our cabin. Wed us with only my family watching. Word still went round, and the next morning Jacob's friends shivareed us here." Hazel blushed.

What did it feel like to wake up to fellars hollering and beating pots and pans? Having to kiss in front of folks, over and over. Would Charlie be willing to accept such, or would he want an English celebration? I hoped I'd find out soon. Hazel stepped near me.

"I feel so blessed sleeping under your coverlets, knowing I'm now kin to such a weaver."

"Thank you." I stared at plump Hazel. Jacob's love had brought fire into her eyes and wiped away the shy girl who had shared a desk with me at school. And she skipped about the cabin showing how she'd claimed it as her nest.

"I'll have to weave extra hard if'n you want coverlets for all those little pallets you and Jacob will fill with young'uns."

"You do that!" Hazel laughed and hugged me. "And I hope the same blessings for you and Charlie."

"Thank you." As I slid my shuttle through the warp's shed I wondered if I was as ready as Hazel to accept the blessings of children.

During dinner, I watched Jacob tease Hazel and how they kept sneaking peeks at each other. Would Charlie lean over and kiss my cheek if he relished the dumplings I had cooked? Hazel and Jacob looked as content as well-fed hogs, and I felt like an intruder. Jacob didn't want any little sister overseeing him and his bride.

I worked until the sun brushed the treetops, and then headed back to the settlement. The English habit of taking afternoon tea, which had at first riled me, offered me another chance to see Charlie. I was thinking about how the sky matched Charlie's eyes when I saw the plumes of smoke.

What fool would light a brush fire with the woods like kindling? Dark puffs billowed above the trees. My mouth went dry. I picked up my skirts and ran. Breaking out of the woods, I gasped.

Flames darted out of the eye of the Tabard. A wave of fire swept across the shake shingles. Hot ashes stung my face. Horses screamed from the stable. Men carrying furniture and carpets raced out of the inn. Mr. Walton and Mr. Hill dragged a large wooden door and propped it in front of a stack of chairs and bedsteads. Mountain folk passed buckets from the stable and heaved them across the stable's roof. Seemed they had already given up on saving the Tabard.

Where was Lizzie? And Charlie? I darted past the crowd and headed for the kitchen door. Seamus and the two stable lads had covered the horses' heads and were leading them down the street. I grabbed Seamus's sleeve.

"Lizzie? Charlie?" I jogged next to Seamus.

"She didn't come out. He went after her." Seamus tied the horse to a hitching post. "Pray, Miss Viney, that he makes it down all those stairs."

"But Lizzie moved! To the second floor!"

"Merciful heavens." Seamus dashed toward the inn, and I followed.

We sprinted to the kitchen. I flung off my apron, ripped it in half, and dunked it in a puddle of water.

"Here, wrap it around your head." I tied my half and ran for the kitchen door.

"Stay out!" Seamus shouted as he covered his head.

"NEVER! You find Charlie."

We crawled up the steps, squinting through the smoke, fighting to breathe. My eyes blurred. Above us the fire roared. Windows exploded. My hands slapped the second-floor landing. The boards were hot, and the thickening smoke squeezed my lungs.

"Go on!" I screamed, and pushed Seamus away. I inched toward Lizzie's door and pushed it open. Every breath hurt. Coughing, I edged into her room.

"Lizzie! Where are you?" Had she left? Fainted? I groped around, but felt nothing. My hands hit her trunk.

Boom! The roof collapsed, and the inn shook. The heat of the boards burned my hands and feet. I pulled myself up.

"Lizzie!" I glanced down. Lizzie lay inside the trunk, curled on top of her wedding gown. I lunged for her.

"Leave be! I ain't comin'. I'm goin' to George." She flailed her legs and arms.

I staggered back, took in one sharp breath, and struck Lizzie's forehead. She shrieked and crumpled. I dug her out of the trunk, heaved her onto my back, and fell to my knees. The landing was a gray square in the heavy smoke. My hands felt the top step. Where were Seamus and Charlie?

Fifteen steps, I told myself. Cinders scorched my feet. Should have worn shoes. Gasping for air, I began to count. One, two . . . five . . . seven steps. Suddenly I knew someone was behind me.

"Hurry," Seamus shouted. "Before . . ."

The third floor slammed onto the second. Plaster dust, smoke, ashes, covered us. I screamed as the stairs swayed. Curtains of fire raced down the walls. Lizzie slipped off my back. Screeching, we rolled over and over. Seamus and Charlie crashed into us, and we fell onto the kitchen floor.

"Crawl!" Seamus shouted.

I pushed Lizzie's limp body in front of me. Would any of

us live? Where was the door? Pain surged across my sides. Vomit rose in my throat.

Seamus tugged on my sleeve with his teeth. I squinted through the gloom. Charlie lay limp on Seamus's back!

"This way." Seamus nudged me.

I rolled Lizzie through a river of smoke. My lungs ached. Dimness swam in front of me. The mudroom door. I dragged Lizzie over the doorsill. Seamus shoved Charlie's body into me, and all of us tumbled onto the steps

Hands lifted us. Voices surrounded us. Someone laid a wet cloth on my head and wrapped my hands and feet.

"Move back!" someone screamed. Men lifted us and ran.

Flames shot skyward. Beams thundered and crashed. The Tabard groaned. Collapsed, smothering us with ashes and dust.

Chapter Twenty-Two

"I can't help feeling and believing that good seed
was sown when Rugby was found, and that
someday the reapers . . . will come along
with joy, bearing heavy sheaves with them."

THOMAS HUGHES

I wanted to cool in the river, to feel the icy current soothing my throbbing hands and feet. Carry me, I tried to beg, but no one answered. My chest ached as if Lizzie had laced me too tightly.

"Take it off." I felt someone's hands. "Hurts."

"Viney," an English voice said. A girl's voice. She bathed my face.

"Unloosen me." I moaned and forced my eyes to open. "Can't breathe." I had seen this girl before.

"Take what off?" She rinsed out the flannel in a china bowl and laid it on my head. "Please tell me."

"Lizzie's corset. Hurts. Lizzie?"

"If you can turn your head a bit, you will see your sister in the bed next to you. She broke her arm. You broke several ribs and are tightly bandaged. Both of you suffered burns, but thank God, nothing worse than reaching for a hot pot without a potholder. Your hair was singed. You were both badly bruised."

Miss Emily Hughes sat next to me, the girl Mr. Thomas Hughes had introduced to us on the day of the library dedication. She looked to be about Lizzie's age and dressed simply, with an apron pinned to her bodice.

"Charlie? Seamus?" I croaked.

"Bruised. Suffering from breathing in smoke, another reason why your lungs hurt and your throat is so sore. Charlie re-injured his shoulder, and Seamus sprained a wrist. Both have burns where cinders seared their clothing. But you are all alive, and no one died in the fire, which is a miracle."

"Where are we?" I looked down at the quilt sewn from hundreds of little hexagons that created a maze of flowers. Paintings hung on the walls paneled with wood, and real lace curtains swayed at the open windows.

"Uffington House, my grandmother's home, down the road from the Tabard. I volunteered to care for you when the doctor said you and Lizzie needed constant nursing. Charlie and Seamus are with the Hills."

"Viney," Lizzie said, "I feared for your head."

"Aches. Everything hurts."

Emily helped Lizzie prop herself against the wooden headboard. A sling held her left arm, and her hair only brushed the collar of her nightgown. Out of the corner of my eye, I could see that my hair fell a few inches below my shoulders.

"The doctor said we should cut your hair. Some of it was

burned, and he thought you would heal faster without the weight." Emily tucked the quilts around Lizzie.

Lizzie reached across the narrow gap and placed her bandaged palm on my muslin-swathed hands. Seeing the wrappings made my heart beat faster. What if our fingers did not heal properly?

"Sister. I'm sorry. Truly."

"Don't fuss. It's all right."

"I think I'll look for a book to read to you two," Emily said, and left the room.

"If'n I had rushed out, none of you would be suffering. 'Twas my foolishness." Tears crept down Lizzie's cheeks. "I might have even saved some of what George gave me, but I lost everything."

"The locket?"

"Snapped off when we fell. Nothing left."

"You have me. And Jacob."

"For a while. But if'n you wed Charlie, you'll be like Jacob and Hazel. Only have eyes for each other."

"I'm different."

"You are, but marriage changes who you think about. What you think on. Loving Charlie has already changed you."

I stared at the white plaster ceiling. Lizzie was right. Although I still grieved for the thickly forested ridge and the herbs churned up by the settlers, those thoughts were a numbness that had slithered into the background of my mind. My hands and heart still yearned for my loom, to feel the smooth wood and smell the wool, but even more, I wanted to see Charlie. I wanted to bake him a pie and together hoe a patch of corn that we had planted. Emily's heels clicked on the wooden floor.

"Have you read *Sense and Sensibility*," she asked. "By Jane Austen? I think you'll enjoy this story."

Lizzie and I listened. In my mind I was Elinor and Charlie was Edward the man I longed to wed.

As soon as the doctor would allow, I begged Emily to help me into a rocker on the porch so that I could sit outside and watch the trees, hear the songbirds. On some days a new lad would drive in with a wagonload of lumber for the rooms Hastings Hughes, Mr. Hughes's brother, was adding to Uffington House. Sometimes Lizzie joined me, but even when I pestered her, she would not sing.

I felt queer sitting in a white muslin dress on an August weekday, not using my hands. Living with these ladies had taught me more about how the English fussed over their women, calling them "delicate creatures," yet Mrs. Hughes could match Aunt Alta in her determination. Dressed in black with a ruffled cap on her head, Mrs. Hughes adored her two little dogs and the new lads drifting into the settlement. But she also ranted at the English press that called Rugby a failure. She wouldn't tolerate folks criticizing her son, Mr. Thomas Hughes.

Swaying on a splint-back rocker, I peered up at the fierce blue sky and prayed that it would pour and drown out the cicadas. Emily opened the screen door, holding a brown envelope.

"Would you like to see my photographs?" she asked, and drew out papers with black-and-white images. I had seen photographs before, but had never met someone who made them.

"How do you create them?" I examined each photograph, hoping to see one of Charlie. Most were of buildings, the Tabard, the Hughes Library, and Christ Church, but she had also caught the faces of some of the lads.

"I use a camera, and different chemicals to develop the images. I suppose it's not all that different from using mordants to set dyes. I was hoping that you would allow me to photograph your weavings."

"My weavings!" My hands paused. All the photographs I had seen were of people and their houses. No one spent cash money taking photographs of weavings.

"You are an artist. Photographs will save what you have created and sold. Something to show your great-grandchildren."

"Thank you." I gulped. "I'd be honored." I picked up the next photograph. Felt queer being called an artist; artists painted.

"Here's one of George. Strange to look at the face of one now in the grave. Lizzie'd relish seeing that one," I said.

"What would I like?" Lizzie walked onto the porch.

"This." Emily handed her the photograph. "It's yours to keep."

Lizzie's eyes puddled. "Thank you. Amazing how you saved his sweet face. I lost his locket in the fire, but now . . ." She wrapped one arm around Emily. "I have this. And I've news, from George's father." She unfolded a letter.

"His father? What did he write?" I scanned Lizzie's face, but she appeared calm.

"His folks are grieving. I had sent them a lock of George's hair. And although they never approved of our engagement, his father wrote that any girl who could convince George to seek marriage and work for a living must be a remarkable young lady." Lizzie's voice trembled. "His pa deeded over a parcel of land here that he had George buy as an investment. Willed the money left in George's Knoxville bank account to me. Said 'God bless.' " Lizzie sank into a chair and leaned back, tears flowing.

"How kind," Emily said. "How very kind. Now you can build the little house you longed for."

"What house?" I asked. From the look exchanged between those two, I knew I had missed some important conversation. Or perhaps I had been too busy in my daydreams about Charlie and had not paid attention?

"We've been talking," Lizzie nodded at Emily. "Isn't fitting to live with Jacob and Hazel, though she'll be needing our help by next spring when the baby arrives. I don't want to live with Aunt Alta and Aunt Idy, too far from the settlement. I'd thought that in a few weeks I could start at the Brown's Boarding House, work until I had enough saved for a cottage and land. Seems the Good Lord took care of me. And you, too." Lizzie looked over at me. "If you want."

"Thank you." But I didn't want to live near the settlement. I yearned for my old home but knew I couldn't share the cabin with Hazel. Things were different.

"Viney, I've been thinking. I'd like to send George's family one of your coverlets. To thank them. To give them a piece of the ridge where he's buried. I would pay you."

"I'd never take your money. You pick out any that you

want. Tell them it's a gift from me, too." I kissed Lizzie's cheek. "For saving me from Robert."

Three weeks later, pink skin covered the burned spots on my hands and I wiggled my fingers. Emily had given me rose-scented cream from England to work into my hands, and they smelled like a June garden. Dressed in a blue calico, I looked like myself as I gazed into Emily's mirror, but I still felt changed, like I had been on a long journey.

"Lizzie, help me with my hair, please?" I asked as I laced my boots.

"Gladly." Her fingers twisted it into a small bun, but even then, a few shorter strands feathered my face.

"If you want to curl those, you can use my curling iron," Emily said.

"Won't take but a minute," Lizzie said. "I'll fix them for you."

Lizzie escorted me to the kitchen, wetted my hair, and twisted it around the iron rod. My hair sizzled a bit and I flinched, recalling the Tabard fire. But when Lizzie released the iron, little curls bounced about my cheeks.

"Makes your face seem even sweeter," she said. "Older."

Old enough to marry, I thought.

Together, the three of us loaded Emily's photography equipment into her grandmother's buggy. Lizzie climbed into the front seat with Emily, but I eased my rear end onto the back seat. My ribs still pained me when I stretched.

"Get up, Nell." Emily slapped the reins. "We'll go look at Lizzie's land first. I sent word out to Hazel that we were stopping by."

I kept my backbone straight and tried to absorb the

bouncing with my legs. It tickled me to ride high up in a buggy, leaving the settlement. Some houses were still boarded up, but folks were going in and out of the commissary, and the rubble had been carted away from the Tabard.

"The Board plans to rebuild in the spring," Emily said. She pulled on the reins, and we turned onto a road that ran down a finger of the ridge that the settlers called Beacon Hill.

"Here," Lizzie said, and we stopped. Lizzie hopped out and gazed about.

"George said we would build a summer home here. Said we would live on Beacon Hill in both Boston and Rugby." A wisp of a smile lightened Lizzie's face.

My heart fluttered. Pink rose into Lizzie's cheeks as she and Emily walked about the property, chattering about where a cottage would have the best views. I leaned against the buggy, cursing my broken ribs.

Emily drove slowly to our old home so as not to stir up the thick dust that smothered the road. Yellow leaves clung to the saplings and brushes, and most of the small plants had withered away. Last September we had storms that flooded Clear Creek, but this year the fall rains held back. I felt a sadness swoop over me when I viewed the roses climbing along the porch railing of our cabin, which could no longer be my home. Yet even Jacob's marriage couldn't scrub away the memories of Lizzie and I teasing each other as we churned or sang on that porch.

"So glad to see y'all up and about," Hazel said, and hugged us. "You'uns make yourselves at home." She ducked her head. "Jacob's needing my help. Pitcher of mint tea in the springhouse." Hazel scurried off toward the corn. Already her body was rounder, filling out with their baby.

"Did you design this?" Emily ran her fingers over the weaving on my loom.

"Yes, I call it 'Viney's Puzzle.' Where do you want to set up your camera?"

"Outside, where there is sufficient light. I'll carry your wheel."

I toted coverlets, and Lizzie carried a patchwork piece she had made. Emily arranged the yarn winder to one side of me and draped a coverlet over the porch railing. She stuck her head beneath a cloth covering her camera, which stood on a wooden tripod, came out and moved everything closer, then looked again. Emily stuck glass plates coated with a silver jelly into the contraption.

"Hold still," Emily called.

My face had stiffened like starched linen before I heard Emily call that she had finished. Lizzie peeked under the cloth, and those two whispered. Finally, Emily fussed with her camera and took a few other photographs before we packed everything up.

"Mrs. Hill invited us to tea," Emily added, and urged the horse toward the Hills'.

Tarnation, I was tired of these two not telling me anything. But I had to confess that most times, I found myself swimming in my thoughts as they chattered. Was this why they curled my hair? My heartbeat quickened when we turned down the Hills' lane. Seamus and Mr. Hill waved from the orchard, and Mrs. Hill wrapped her arms around me.

"Charlie's in the barn," she whispered. "Why don't you tell him that tea will be ready soon."

My feet wanted to fly, but my innards felt shy. My heart kept thumping against those tingling ribs. I opened the barn door. Charlie sat in the shade of the loft, with his head slumped against the boards of the stall. A harness he must have been mending had fallen from his hands. His cheekbones pinched his pale face, and the skin on his fingers was slick where the burns had healed. I knelt down next to him and kissed his cheek.

"Charlie, I miss you."

Slowly Charlie dragged his eyes open. "Viney." He reached over and gently pulled me close. "Oh, how I have missed you. How are your ribs? Your hands?"

"Mending." I snuggled my head on his chest, listening to his heartbeat and breathing in the scent of leather and horses. Charlie inhaled deeply.

"You smell like my mother's rose garden." Charlie kissed my palms. "I was dreaming I was home, standing in a mist, listening to the sea. What I would give for one afternoon in a cool green field." He brushed his cheek against my hand.

With me, I wanted to add, but instead I said, "Mrs. Hill says tea's ready."

"You're staying?" Charlie lifted me to my feet.

"Yes," I answered. "Along with Lizzie and Emily."

Charlie offered me his arm, and we walked to the house.

Mrs. Hill, Emily, and Lizzie prattled on during tea. Seamus and Mr. Hill only sat for a short while and then went back to farming. But before Mr. Hill walked away, I saw him wink at

Charlie, whose hand had found mine beneath the tablecloth. If only we could be alone.

"Grandmother asked if all of you would please share dinner with us on Sunday?" Emily said, and folded her napkin.

"Yes, thank you," Mrs. Hill said. "I'm sure the menfolk will be pleased, too."

"Good. Thank you for the lovely tea, but we should be going." Emily glanced at the clock on the mantle.

"Thank you," Lizzie and I said, and we gathered up the empty plates and teacups.

Charlie brought around the buggy and helped me into the back seat. I did not want his hands to leave my waist.

"'Till Sunday," he whispered.

"'Till Sunday," I repeated, and waved as we drove away.

The long shadows of the trees flickered across the buggy as we rolled up the road. Above the fall of the horses' hooves, I heard the chipping evening call of the redbird and realized how weary I was from the traveling. Emily turned the team onto the two-track leading to Aunt Idy and Aunt Alta's cabin.

"Can't dally," Lizzie said, "But we need to see how the aunts be. Haven't visited since before the typhoid struck."

Her words pinched me. These past weeks I hadn't thought much about our aunts. I frowned when we saw the darkened cabin, but we found Aunt Alta rocking on the front porch. As wrinkled as a black walnut, and hunkered down in her chair, she looked like a child's doll.

"Come on up." Aunt Alta waved to us.

"You're alone," Lizzie said.

"Where's Aunt Idy?" I asked. "Like you to meet our friend, Emily Hughes."

"Pleased to make your acquaintance, ma'am." Emily took Aunt Alta's hand. "I am Mr. Hughes's niece."

"Pleased to meet you. My, my, three fair young ladies out riding."

"Where's Idy?" Lizzie repeated.

"Gone to Jamestown. Her granddaughter's husband fetched Idy to help with a birthin'. Idy's daughter talkin' about Idy staying on for the winter. Wants to bring me to her cabin, too. Don't think two old women should live out here alone no more."

"But you didn't go." I said. The dark was creeping in as the sun sank behind the ridge. Aunt Alta was another hard-headed Walker, as close to a mother as Lizzie and I had known.

"Nope. Ain't goin'. I'll trust in the Good Lord and get by." Aunt Alta's gnarled hands gripped the arms of her rocker. "Unless one of you lambs would like to winter with this old ewe."

I slipped into the cabin and lit a lamp. The flame sputtered and smoked, as the wick needed trimming. The fire on the hearth smoldered, and a layer of grease shone on the pot of beans. How long had those beans stood in that pot? Dust balls rolled beneath the table. I bit my lip while I stirred up the fire and moved the kettle closer. Lizzie opened the door, and Emily escorted Aunt Alta to the table.

"I'll stay for a day or two." My voice quavered, watching Aunt Alta shuffle by. Truth was, it might be weeks before I could leave. "You be needing help."

"Are you certain?" Lizzie asked.

"Certain. I'll sleep in my chemise tonight. Send Jacob by tomorrow with my belongings."

"But Charlie," Lizzie whispered in my ear.

"Aunt Alta needs taking care of *now*." I spoke low. "Can't be any wedding until I'm asked. Room here for my loom." Thoughts snapped inside my head, sending out sparks.

I watched the dark shape of the buggy fade into the forest as the whip-poor-wills sawed out their names. I inhaled the rich scent of leaves and of the hemlocks surrounding the cabin. Leaving Rugby felt like shucking Lizzie's corset. Tomorrow I would set up my loom and throw my shuttle across the warp, feeling the threads hum. Lizzie's land near the settlement would never match the peace of this clearing. There would always be the rumble of wagons and the screech of the sawmill near her cabin. But this scrap of land held the sweetness and strength of the mountains.

CHAPTER TWENTY-THREE

*In the mountains the need is for development not foreign
to our natures, cultivation of talents already in blossom.
Let us be given work that will make us better
mountaineers, instead of turning us into poor
imitation city folk.*

EMMA BELL MILES, *The Spirit of the Mountains*

Sunday morning I brushed Aunt Alta's hair and wound it into a bun. Lizzie had bought me pink cambric from the same bolt that I had chosen for that silly gown, and I had sewn a new churchgoing dress. But come winter, I vowed to weave fabric for another blue-checked dress.

"Right pretty in pink frock," Aunt Alta said. "Still trying to capture that young fellar's heart? Tie the knot?"

"Well, Charlie says he cares . . . but he's slow to talk about marriage." I braided my hair and pinned it up.

"Are you willing to leave everything for him, child? Like Lizzie? Your fellar might be wondering if you would forsake even weaving for him?" Aunt Alta's gnarled fingers slipped over mine. "Would you?"

"I'll never give up weaving. It's like breathing." My hands trembled. Babies might slow me a mite, but somehow I would find a way.

"Besides, Charlie understands." I glanced at the cream and brown coverlet I had been weaving these past days. "He would never want me to stop weaving."

"If'n that's true, you best wed that boy." Aunt Alta's eyes danced. "Bring him back here. Empty cabin needs shoutin' children; that pasture full of weeds could use a man's hands."

"Charlie?" I'd never thought of us buying the aunts' farm.

"Is there another?" Aunt Alta cackled. "Ain't the same without Idy. Y'all could set up housekeeping here. I'm good at rockin' babies."

"A farm for us . . . " I hugged Aunt Alta until she shooed me away.

"Where did I leave my cane?" She tottered to her feet. "Time for the preachin'."

With Aunt Alta holding on to my arm and leaning on her cane, I guided her down the porch steps, where Jacob and Hazel waited in their new wagon that Lizzie had bought them.

"Come along?" Jacob asked as he helped Aunt Alta into the wagon. "Folks say there might even be a baptism. Preacher Giles down from Kentucky."

"No, thank you. I'll go on to church with Lizzie."

Carrying my stockings and boots, I walked toward the settlement. Dust coated the sassafras leaves, which had turned yellow. Charlie had told me that only a quarter of an inch of rain had fallen in the past ten weeks. We needed a week of rain to wash away the grime and revive the settlement's puny tomato crop. My feet sank into thick dust as if it was warm, gritty snow. I smelled horses and heard the jingle of harness. A buggy rounded the curve.

"Viney!" Mrs. Hill called. "You'll spoil that frock. Please join us."

"Whoa," Mr. Hill said, and halted the buggy by the side of the road.

Charlie lifted me in, and I arranged my skirts and petticoats so as not to show dirty feet. I relished feeling the brush of his shoulder against mine.

"Where's Seamus?" I asked.

"He practices the Roman Catholic faith. A priest from Knoxville wrote him and said he was stopping by Sedgemore this Sunday. Seamus rode over. He should be home by supper." Charlie spread a dust robe across my lap. "Barometer's falling," he added.

I stared at the excitement in his face.

"That means it might *rain*. Barometric pressure fell to twenty-nine point six. Heat feels different, too, heavier."

Charlie was right. Here it was early morning and my dress already clung to me. Under the dust cover Charlie's fingers locked with mine.

"Would you sit with me in the Hill's pew?" Charlie whispered.

"Yes." I could feel the barometer of my heart rise. When a fellar sat with his girl during the preaching, folks reckoned the courting was serious. Quicker than a fox, the buggy rolled up to Christ Church. I pulled my feet beneath the cover and whipped on both stockings and boots. Charlie offered me his arm, and I felt like everyone watched as we marched down the aisle.

Although I had come to Christ Church a few times with Lizzie and Emily, I never could remember when to stand or kneel. Charlie opened a little black book.

"From my uncle. Follow along."

I forced myself to listen to the preacher. But my eyes relished the colors scattered across the church from the stained glass windows. I wondered if I could find a way to weave so many colors into such a fine pattern of light.

Finally, the service ended, and Charlie and I, plus Lizzie and Emily, strolled back to Uffington House. Charlie and Emily talked about places in England they both knew, and I felt like I was the foreigner. If she'd been some other girl, I would have fussed over her attentions to Charlie, but I trusted Emily.

It felt queer to have Charlie push in my chair, and to once again sit at a cloth-covered table set with silver candlesticks. The starched lace curtains filtered the sunlight into hundreds of freckles that dotted the linen. Emily had arranged a bouquet of asters and goldenrod, and even set out crystal goblets. Although I had eaten Sunday dinner on fancy china for several weeks, we'd had no guests. Mrs. Hughes took a seat at one end of the long table, and Mr. Hill occupied the other. Charlie sat across from me and kept fiddling with his fork. Lizzie insisted upon helping the cook carry in the platters of roast chicken, plus bowls of mashed potatoes and green beans with bacon.

After Mr. Hughes asked the blessings, everyone ate and chattered, except Charlie. He shoveled in his food like it was to be his last meal, and I kept hoping to feel his foot nudge mine. When the last crumbs of chocolate cake were wiped away, Lizzie and Emily offered to wash dishes. Charlie cleared his throat.

"Shall we go for a walk?" He glanced at the open window. The air was as thick as a wet fleece, and no breeze rippled the curtains.

"Yes, please." I saw that Emily and Lizzie were watching us as they cleared the table. My heart flip-flopped when Charlie pulled out my chair.

"Viney." Emily put a hand on my arm. "A minute please." She pulled me toward her room.

"Proper ladies wear a bonnet." She placed on my head her straw bonnet lined with sage green silk and tied a matching silk ribbon under my chin. "And gloves. Here rub on more rose water and glycerin first." She handed me a pair of lace mitts.

I stared at the mitts, thinking about the dedication of the library. "Thank you. The bonnet will keep off that miserable sun, but it's too hot for gloves."

Charlie waited, wearing his straw boater. He slipped his arm thought mine, and we wandered down a graveled path heading toward the river. Although the bonnet shaded my face, it blocked my view of Charlie.

"Do you know what Mr. Hughes named this path?" Charlie asked, and slipped his arm around my waist. "The Lovers' Walk."

We bowed under a low-hanging branch and ambled toward the sound of the White River. I could find no words for what coursed through me. I loved the weight of his arm around me, but Emily's bonnet hindered me from snuggling my head against Charlie's chest. I pulled on the ribbons, and they snarled.

"May I?" Charlie leaned over and worked out the knot. As the bonnet fell back his lips covered mine. I was as hungry for that kiss as the land yearned for rain.

"Viney, I have no land, yet. But when I do, will you marry me?" Charlie asked.

"I'd marry you this moment." I brushed my cheek against his rough one. "Land doesn't matter."

"Maybe to you, but a man must be able to support a wife. Even one who sells her weavings." Charlie held my face in his hands.

I saw George cupping Lizzie's face with his fingers. I moved to kiss Charlie, but he shook his head.

"Listen, please, for just a moment." His thumbs brushed my cheeks.

I gazed into those gentian blue eyes. My cheeks tingled at his touch. How could I listen when all I wanted was kissing?

"Wednesday, I am leaving with Seamus to work in Michigan."

"What!" I started to step back, but Charlie's hands slid to my waist and held me fast.

"Please. Listen. For now, Seamus and I will pick apples on Mr. Hill's old farm near Traverse City. Come November the two of us will work for a lumber company on Beaver Island."

They were leaving me. I tasted salt trickling across my lips.

"But you asked me to marry you!"

"When I own land. I can't stay here this winter. I can earn more money with these jobs so that I can buy our farm sooner. And Mr. Hill's old farm rides a sandy ridge where I can climb the hills and watch storms move across Lake Michigan. I need to hear waves again."

What if that northern land claimed his heart? "Please don't go. Wait, please. I have an idea."

Charlie pulled away. "Listen a bit more. I heard from my father."

"So? What does that have to do with *us*?" My tears blurred his face.

"Mr. Hill wrote him when I was hurt. Father wrote back. Said time had calmed him, plus his concern over my injuries. He admitted that if I was keen on farming, then I should stay in America. He even offered to loan me money to buy land, but not in Rugby. The English press keeps writing about the failure of the settlement. He thinks I must settle somewhere else."

"But what if you *could* farm here? I'm staying with Aunt Alta. She offered us her farm. It needs a man. We could wed now." Far off, I heard the growl of thunder.

"I don't think I can live through another long, dry southern summer, watching plants die. Your aunt's offer is kind, but until I visit Michigan, I can't accept it. I must see what that land is like. And the man who bought Mr. Hill's farm is talking of selling. Please, over the winter, think about maybe moving north?"

Thunder rumbled, and the ground vibrated. A breeze tickled the treetops. Birds flew into the shelter of bushes.

"*Rain*," we said, and looked up at the swaying branches. Thick gray clouds scuttled overhead.

"We'd better head back." Charlie took my hand, and we hastened along the path as the sky darkened.

The storm inside me rose and battered against my heart. With each clap of thunder, I heard Aunt Alta asking me if I was willing to give up everything for this man, even these hills. Fat drops of rain hit our faces and splattered in the dust.

"The library," Charlie said, and we ran.

Lightning cracked. Thunder roared. A gray curtain swept across the hills. We dashed up the porch steps just as the clouds opened and rain pounded the tin roof. Leaning against the wall, Charlie pulled me back toward him and rested his chin on my head. He locked his hands around my waist.

"Isn't it beautiful?" he shouted about the rushing wind and sheets of rain. "Bet my barometer fell to SQUALLS AND CLEARING. Probably rising as we watch. Feel the wind shifting to the north?"

Spray from the downpour blew across the porch, cooling my face. I gazed at the flow of the ridge blurred by the veil of rain. How could I even think of leaving my home? And what about Lizzie, who still cried at George's grave? Or Aunt Alta, who could no longer live alone?

"A north wind." Charlie whirled me around to face him. "Please say that you will consider my proposal. That you'll give me your answer in the spring?"

"Yes." I pulled his head down and locked my arms around his neck. I kissed Charlie with all the power the mountains gave me, and his lips lingered. The thunder rumbled from the east as the storm moved beyond the ridge. The tree frogs sang praises. Finally, the clip-clop of a horse separated us. A buggy plodded down the road.

"Charlie! Viney!" Seamus stuck his head out of an isinglass window. "I've been searching for you. Hop in!"

We ran through the puddles. Charlie lifted me in and climbed into the back seat. I snuggled against him and never wanted to part. Rain pattered against the leather roof. Seamus turned around and eyed us.

"You'll be forgiving me for taking Charlie north?"

"I reckon. Though I hope *both* of you return."

"I cannot speak for Charlie, but I belong with me own people. My mother's cousin invited us up. Many Irish live on Beaver Island." Seamus clucked to the horse. "Off to your aunt's now."

Rain trickled down the translucent windows while Seamus whistled a jig. I could feel Charlie's heartbeat beneath his soaked shirt. I shivered, and Charlie hugged me closer.

"We'll have you home soon." He brushed away the hair that had come loose from my bun. "A cup of tea, a dry frock, and you'll be warm."

Home to Aunt Alta, but not home with you, I wanted to say. But instead I cuddled closer. Only two more days and his arms would no longer warm me.

The night before Charlie departed, he rode up to Aunt Alta's cabin and tied the Hills' mare to a tree. We cuddled on the bottom porch step, our arms around each other. As the sky darkened, stars blossomed. A screech owl's call shivered through the clearing.

"I brought you something," Charlie said. "In my country gentlemen give their fiancé a special ring."

"Fiancée?" I flipped my tongue about the foreign word.

"French for the betrothed person." Charlie handed me a small muslin poke. "I know that ours is more of an understanding, but I wanted you to have something precious of mine. And it is round."

I pulled out his aneroid barometer. "You can't give me this! How will you mind the coming weather?"

"'Tis mine to give." Charlie cocked his head. "And when the north winds blow and the needle rises, think of me sending my love. Hoping to convince you that wherever I farm, you will join me."

"And when the needle falls, I suppose that's because I'll be here, fussing at you for leaving me?"

"Every time I feel a wind from the south, I'll listen for your voice." Charlie leaned over and kissed me.

His kiss was like lemonade, full of his sweetness and the bitterness of parting. Feeling the heat rising in me, I pushed him aside.

"You be needing something to remind you of *me*." I stepped into the cabin and brought out the coverlet I had designed for Charlie.

"Here. Named the pattern "Bright Spells and Showers." Big enough to cover two someday." I swiped at the tears inching down my cheeks.

"Thank you." Charlie rocked me in his arms. "Every night I will dream of you."

I snuffled and shook, sobbing until his shirt grew soggy. Charlie pulled out his handkerchief and pressed it into my palm. "Here. It's clean."

"How many of these have you given me?" I blew my nose and wiped my eyes, but the tears wouldn't stop.

"Enough, I hope, to tie your heart to mine. 'Tis late, and the train comes early."

Charlie pulled me to my feet, and we linked arms around each other's waists as we walked to his horse. He cupped my face in his weathered hands and kissed me until my knees melted. I lowered my head onto the fine golden hair showing at his open collar and I breathed in the scent of his flesh, like the damp soil beneath my bare feet. I wanted to hold him forever.

"I'll write as soon as I arrive." Charlie rubbed his cheek against mine. "Work with your hands. Weave." With one last kiss he mounted his horse with my coverlet under his arm and rode away.

Leaning against a tree, I sobbed until I sank to the ground. High above, stars glittered in a wave of silver lace. Only the screech owl spoke through the rustling of the leaves. I clenched handfuls of dirt, and the loamy scent filled my nose. My toes curled deep into the soil, feeling the rhythm of the mountain's heartbeat. Tonight I couldn't imagine ever leaving the ridge, but I knew that a piece of me would depart when Charlie boarded the train. And who knows what I might have to do to seal our love? I was no longer the girl who had cursed the foreigners as she rescued healing plants; that same girl would never have dreamed of sending her weavings across an ocean. Nor that she would create a coverlet for a man she loved. I closed my eyes.

Tomorrow my hands would card and spin. I would fill shuttles and cast them across the warp, delighting in the whack of the beater and the rattle of the harnesses. I would dream and pray for the spring day when Charlie would return. To once again share the work of our hands.

Author's Note

Viney Walker is based on a real person, Dicey Fletcher, who lived in the Cumberland Mountains where the Rugby colonists settled. Miss Fletcher was an independent woman who dedicated her life to weaving and never married; her decision displayed an unusual artistic determination in nineteenth-century Appalachian culture, where marriage and motherhood were the expected goals. Samples of Miss Fletcher's weavings are housed in the Cincinnati Museum of Art, and I thank Cindy Armeaus for showing me Dicey's work. Other characters in the novel were also people who walked Rugby's dusty streets; Jacob and Lizzie, Amos and Margaret Hill, Thomas, Hastings, Emily and Madame Hughes shared Rugby's past glory. Charlie, Seamus, George, Susanna, and Robert represent the various young men and ladies who came to the colony for different reasons.

Between 1880 and 1890, the Board of Aid to Land Owners owned 75,000 acres along the ridge, and Rugby drew settlers from America and England. The colony's population peaked at 450 in 1884. Many of the buildings were built according to Andrew Jackson Downing's architectural designs, which promoted simple, practical cottages. Visitors may tour several of the original buildings such as Christ Church Chapel, Uffington House, Thomas Hughes's home Kingstone Lisle, and the Hughes Library, which houses a unique collection of Victorian books.

Rugby failed to survive as a utopian community for several reasons. The Board continued to squabble over how to divide and sell its title property, and this confusion resulted in long delays and frustrations for the men who wanted to buy land. Because the

Board resided in London, communication between the colony and England was a problem.

The soil was not as fertile as the Rugby Handbook advertised, therefore farms did not yield the lush crops it promised. During the colony's first year, the residents endured a severe winter, and a terrible drought that limited the harvest. The local railroad never built a promised track that would have linked Rugby with Sedgemore; therefore shipping the colony's products to larger cities remained a problem because of the rough and winding mountain roads. Typhoid fever scattered the residents and left only a few to carry the load. Once the threat was over, a fair population trickled back into Rugby, but further trials continued to erode the confidence of the English press. Yet, another larger conflict prompted the colony's demise.

Most of the Englishmen came from a background where they were not trained in manual labor and had never worked. They were deposited in a wilderness, hours from the closest village, without any knowledge of how to farm. Building houses, plowing land, weeding acres of crops, caring for animals is demanding work, and the lads were not prepared mentally or physically for these jobs. That they succeeded as well as they did is an amazing testimony to their resolve and the men who led the community.

In 1884 the Tabard Inn burned; for the sake of my story I placed this event in the same summer as the epidemic. The inn was rebuilt, but the second also burned, so Rugby could no longer depend upon the tourist income. After Madame Hughes died in 1887, the colony continued to dwindle, and the English and American press declared it a failure. Some colonists did remain in the Cumberland Mountains.

Tension existed between the settlers and the mountaineers, who complained about the colonists' demand that they pen their hogs and about the settlement driving away the game. Most mountaineers lived on small subsistence farms and hunted for additional food. While they would have appreciated the cash they could earn and the settlement's commissary, many of the English manners would have appeared frivolous. One person whose ancestors lived near Rugby said that her great-uncle told stories about the "haughty and arrogant" Englishmen who invaded their hills.

Hopefully, this story has sparked interest in various areas, and I have included a list and description of websites where readers may learn more about Rugby, weaving, traditional music, and Downing architecture.

www.historicrugby.org displays photos of many of the buildings mentioned, plus includes a lengthy biography about Thomas Hughes and additional information concerning present-day activities at Historic Rugby, such as their Christmas program.

www.hindmansettlement.org is the website for the Hindman Settlement School, which was founded over a hundred years ago in Knott County, Kentucky, and offers an Appalachian Family Folk Week during June where all ages can learn more about Appalachian culture, especially music and dance such as Viney enjoyed.

www.folkschool.com is the website for the John C. Campbell Folk School, located near Brasstown, North Carolina. The Folk School schedules classes in weaving, music, and dance, and is another beautiful setting where readers can discover more about folk arts.

www.comhaltas.ie is the website for Comhaltas Ceoltoiri Eireann, the traditional music and dance society of Ireland, which has branches across the United States and in other countries, where people gather to study instruments such as fiddle and harp or to learn Irish dancing. Seamus would have loved the jam sessions sponsored by Comhaltas!

GLOSSARY

Alum: potassium aluminum sulfate, a chemical commonly used as a *mordant* to set dyes. Sometimes alum can be mined near the surface of the earth, such as at Alum Cave Bluff in the Great Smoky Mountains.

Beater: the part of a loom that is moved back and forth to pack the weft after a *shuttle* is thrown. The beater holds the *reed*.

Breast beam: the wooden bar at the front of the loom above the cloth roller and parallel to the *reed*. The finished cloth passes over the breast beam as it is rolled onto the cloth roller.

Cookstove: a large cast-iron stove fueled by a wood fire that both heats the oven and flows under the top surface where pots sit. The intensity of the fire is controlled by small doors that allow air to feed the blaze. Also different types of wood produce varying amounts of heat.

Copper sulfate: a green copper powder used as a *mordant* to stabilize green dyes. Sometimes known as copperas.

Curds: the thick casein-rich particles of milk formed either by souring milk or adding rennet. Most people are familiar with small or large curd cottage cheese.

Harness: the wooden frames holding the *heddles*. The harnesses are raised and lowered by working the foot peddles.

Heddles: cord or wire loops attached to the bars connected to the *harness*. The *warp* threads run through the *heddles*. When *warping* a loom, you pull the thread through the eye of a *heddle,* then through the *reed*, before attaching the thread to the main *breast beam*.

Least one: a term defining the youngest member in the family, usually a baby or toddler.

Modal: refers to various arrangements of the eight diatonic notes. For example, in the Dorian mode the notes of the key of D are arranged on the second degree of a major scale, so the tune sounds as if it is played in a minor key. The sea chanty *The Drunken Sailor* is a good example of the Dorian mode.

Mordant: a chemical that fixes a dye so that the color will not fade.

Mortise: a rectangular hole, or a slot, in a piece of timber, filled by the *tenon*.

Red oil: a salve created from the Saint-John's-wort flower and lousewort steeped in oil. Viney would have used lard.

Reed: comblike part of a loom used to separate the *warp* threads evenly.

Scourge: a widespread affliction, a term used by the mountaineers to define a particular summer illness.

Shuttle: the boat-shaped tool that holds the thread that is placed between the *warp* threads. A weaver throws a *shuttle* through the *warp*, whacks it in place with the *beater*, and then hits the next foot peddle before throwing the *shuttle* again.

Switchel: a drink made of water, molasses or maple syrup, and ginger. *Switchel* quenches thirst better than plain water.

Tenon: the tongue-shaped wedge of wood chiseled at the end of a beam. When using post and beam construction, the *tenon* fits into the *mortise* and forms the framework of a building or of large loom.

Warp: the threads that run along the loom. The *warp* is raised and lowered by the harness and the foot peddles.

Warping board: four boards screwed together in the form of a rectangle. Pegs are attached to the boards at certain intervals. When measuring a *warp*, the weaver runs the threads around the pegs.